The Queen's Shadow

The Chanters Novellas: Book 1

Rachel Song

Songbird Publishing

Copyright © 2024 by Rachel Song

All rights reserved.

No part of this publication may be reproduced, distributed, or transmitted in any form or by any means, including photocopying, recording, or other electronic or mechanical methods, without the prior written permission of the publisher, except as permitted by U.S. copyright law. For permission requests, contact Rachel Song at rachelsongauthor.com.

The story, all names, characters, and incidents portrayed in this production are fictitious. No identification with actual persons (living or deceased), places, buildings, and products is intended or should be inferred.

Book Cover by Rachel Song

To my husband Mike,
for his constant support and encouragement

Contents

1. Chapter 1 — 1
2. Chapter 2 — 14
3. Chapter 3 — 26
4. Chapter 4 — 41
5. Chapter 5 — 54
6. Chapter 6 — 72
7. Chapter 7 — 90
8. Chapter 8 — 103
9. Chapter 9 — 121

Epilogue — 140

Acknowledgements — 147

About the Author — 149

Chapter 1

The palace courtyard was bathed in the glow of enchanted orb fire, and up in the eaves, Cassandra Macia nocked an arrow.

Below, the courtiers whirled and laughed and danced as she pulled the bowstring taut and took aim at the man's back. She hesitated, daring him to look up at her. It would be far less fun if he didn't see her at all.

He turned suddenly, his eyes finding her easily, as if he'd known she were there.

He winked.

Damn.

Arphaxad's mouth tipped beneath his silver, fox-shaped mask in that annoying way he had when he knew he'd won, as if daring her to let the arrow loose.

Her fingers twitched. She could still release the arrow, still stick to the plan—not that it had even been part of the plan to begin with. She lowered her bow, then slid the arrow back in its quiver, careful not to touch the poisoned tip. Briar root on a blunt tip wouldn't kill, but its effects weren't exactly pleasant either. And a blunt arrow from her bow would hurt. A lot.

She smirked at the thought as she slung her bow across her shoulders, then looked back to where he had stood among the masked dancers. It was the height of the summer solstice, and blues and greens and pinks flashed in quick succession as the dance concluded, ripples of laughter and applause for the band rising into the warm night air.

Arphaxad was gone.

Cassandra's mouth tipped down as she slunk along the eaves of the palace. What was wrong with her tonight? She was supposed to be one of the queen's best—"as silent as the night and as swift as an arrow," the people of Rendra said. But he was repeatedly the one man she could never get the best of. And it made her mad.

She slipped silently to the ground at the edge of the palace, stashing her bow and the quiver of poisoned arrows beneath a carefully-trimmed hedge. A stately foxtrot blazed to life in the courtyard behind her, accompanied by tinkling laughter. The night was clear, and she could make out the constellation of Asaragus the Archer gleaming to the north—the sign of Rendra's queen.

Her chest tightened. She couldn't fail tonight. She wouldn't fail. Whatever Arphaxad thought he knew of her, of Rendra's queen, she would prove him wrong.

And now that he knew she was here, there was only one way out—and it involved doing something incredibly, stupidly reckless.

She pulled her mask shaped like a sleek black cat firmly over her face, smoothing her dark hair in its knot at the back of her head. It was not as fashionably done as Medira's other courtiers, but everything about her, from her hair to her gown of nondescript dark blue, had been fashioned to be forgettable.

Cassandra was well-trained in the art of being forgettable. It was an essential part of being the queen's shadow. And with her olive skin and thick brown hair, it was easy to blend in among the populations of both Rendra and Medira, populations that shared a language and an ancestral history. But not much more than that—at least not lately.

She threw her shoulders back and strode confidently past the guards dressed in the green and red of Medira—their plumed helmets giving them the look of ceremonial peacocks—along the black stone path lighted by the yellow glow of enchanted orb fire, and into the licentiously decorated courtyard. The guards hardly spared her a glance.

Elegantly dressed men and women filled the space that was usually reserved for receiving carriages or for displays of military prowess. The Mediran king had already retired for the night, leaving his court to carouse without him.

Cassandra kept her back to the wall as she circled the courtyard, her eyes moving. Arphaxad knew she was here now, alone in the enemy's court. She was being bold, brazen even, stepping into the courtyard like this, but right now, she didn't care.

Something pressed against the small of her back, something sharp and metallic, and then a voice, deep and familiar, sounded in her ear. "May I have this dance, my lady?"

A thrill went through her, and Cassandra's lips curved in a smile. "You know I can never say no to you."

The knife pressed more firmly against her back, and she hissed, but then the pressure disappeared, and she turned to look up into the twinkling brown eyes of Arphaxad Ilin Serra, the nephew of the king of Medira. A nephew who was so far down the line of succession that it was extremely unlikely he would ever ascend the throne—which put him in the perfect position to head the king's intelligence division.

He wasn't as tall as she had expected the first time they had met almost five years ago, not long after her twentieth birthday, when she had taken over for the former shadow. But he was taller than her, though not much older, and he had used that height to his advantage in the past—something she had quickly learned never to let him do again.

He held out a sun-darkened hand. She hesitated before taking it, then turned her face up and smiled brilliantly beneath her mask. His expression was unreadable beneath his own mask, but his dark eyes flashed back at her. Suddenly, the music started up—a lilting, lively waltz—and they swept into the fray.

Cassandra never felt more alive than when their game was on.

"How fitting," Arphaxad drawled as they joined the cascade of whirling couples. "A shadow on the day the shadows are shortest."

"A small shadow can slip in anywhere," she returned, "like a black cat in the night."

"Ha," Arphaxad said. His hand pressed into the small of her back, but the knife from before had disappeared. "You know, shadows are more than just bedtime stories used to frighten rebellious children."

Cassandra did know. There were rumors of old magics powerful enough to tear from their world into a realm of shadow and let the things that lived there through. Rumors that weren't as unfounded as most people wanted to believe.

"How did you know I was here?" she asked without breaking his gaze.

"You're encroaching on my territory," he said. "I know everything that goes on here."

Cassandra snorted. "Of course you do."

"I'm surprised you even tried something so juvenile as that trick with the bow." He leaned toward her, and his heady, earthy scent wafted over her. "What's your real play, Cass?"

Cass. The name he called her to get under her skin.

"My real play?" She laughed. "You know I only came here to see you, Phax."

His mouth twisted at the name she used to get under his skin.

"Of course." He raised their arms suddenly, spinning her out as the music swelled. When he pulled her back in, they were closer than before, and she could feel the warmth of him through her gown. "This visit has nothing to do with the presence of the Inetian ambassador, does it? I'm sure your queen is gnashing her teeth at the thought of a Mediran and Inetian alliance."

Gnashing her teeth. That was an understatement. The Rendran queen had been livid when she'd heard of the ambassador's presence at the palace. It was yet another betrayal from the Mediran king. Medira and Rendra had had a tenuous relationship since the Mediran king had broken part of their trade alliance eighteen years earlier, not long after the queen had taken over for her father. He had violated Rendra's trust repeatedly in the following years, but this was something else entirely.

Cassandra gave Arphaxad her sweetest smile. "The Inetian ambassador, you say? I hear there's an Inetian princess of marriageable age, though I can't imagine a teenager would much like being married to a man well into his fifties, even if he is a king."

"Indeed." Arphaxad's fingers tightened at her back. "You clearly know everything already. What other information could you possibly want from me?"

She gave him a tight smile. "It seems we are at an impasse, then."

"Are we ever truly at an impasse, Cass?" he drawled.

She simply smiled.

The waltz sped up then, and Cassandra's heartbeat quickened as they whirled in ever tightening circles, and she did her best not to let her feet get tangled. Arphaxad was an adept dancer, but so was she. It was all part of the job, to move and dance and fight like she wasn't there at all. She would not let him outdo her.

She followed where he led, one hand against his shoulder, the other placed in his, the space between them so small yet also a chasm neither would dare cross. She kept her eyes on him, on the curve of his jaw, the dark stubble that lined it, on the glint in his eyes, at once dangerous and electrifying.

She was squarely in enemy territory, in a place where he could call for the guards at any moment. But that wasn't how this game was played. Not with him. She would be sorely disappointed if it were.

The music rose again in a final, wild crescendo and then dropped away as suddenly as it had started. Applause echoed into the night air, but neither Cassandra nor Arphaxad moved. Something flashed in his gaze that Cassandra couldn't quite read. A moment passed and then another, a strange expectation hovering between them. Then finally, Arphaxad was stepping away, and Cassandra found herself feeling drained and strangely disappointed.

"This way, my lady," Arphaxad said, his voice holding a formality it hadn't a moment before.

She followed him to the edge of the courtyard where a large green-and-red banner fluttered in the night breeze. They made their way through a narrow stone archway and down into a sunken garden. The pink versithia were in full bloom, and their sweet scent almost overpowered the space.

"Are you taking me to see your king?" Cassandra asked, keeping her voice carefully light.

Arphaxad's mouth quirked. "Your queen would like that, wouldn't she?"

He stepped up to a small door at the edge of the garden. He reached under his black tunic and drew out a ring of keys. He used one to unlock the door and pulled it open. A rough staircase disappeared upward into darkness.

"After you," he said, gesturing toward the open door.

Cassandra gave Arphaxad a quick smile as she stepped up beside him. She was so close she could make out the beads of sweat sliding down his neck from the heat. "How about we go my way instead," she said, pressing a knife into his side.

Arphaxad blinked. "You—" he stuttered, reaching for the knife that was no longer on his person.

"I what?" She grinned. "I thought you were trained to expect the unexpected."

"This is still my territory, Cass," Arphaxad said, his voice low, dangerous.

"But I am the queen's shadow," she said, leaning up so her mouth was next to his ear. She thought she felt him shiver.

"You can be insufferable, you know," he said. There was no hint of frustration in his tone, only amusement.

"I don't think I'm alone in that," she returned with a smirk.

Arphaxad moved in front of her as she guided him through the garden, his knife still at his back, his face unreadable beneath his mask in the darkness. She could hear his breathing in the stillness of the night, imagine him running through scenarios to get himself out of this. The rest of the court was either attending the ball, reveling in the midsummer night, or asleep.

They reached the edge of the palace quickly—too quickly. The Mediran capital stretched out below them, whitewashed villas descending toward smaller, wooden structures the farther from the palace one went. The faint orange glow of hundreds of bonfires dotted the edge of Lake Enterra as the people of Medira celebrated the longest day of the year. White-capped mountains glimmered in the distance, marking the border with Rendra at the center of the peninsula.

Cassandra was struck by the familiarity of it all. She could picture the bonfires taking place now across Rendra too. She could imagine people singing the folksongs of her childhood and holding contests to see who could jump the farthest across the flames. She could envision her queen laughing with her closest advisors as they drank sweet wine from Trenta, the night air bringing with it the promise of a good harvest.

Something twisted in Cassandra's chest. The two lands weren't so different after all.

"So, what now?" Arphaxad asked.

Cassandra's grip tightened on Arphaxad's knife. The two kingdoms were different enough.

"It's time for you to sleep," she said. A heady exhilaration laced with unease thundered through her body. This had all been too easy.

"Sleep?" Arphaxad said, but his words were already slurred. The briar root was already working. He would be out shortly and would wake hours later with a nasty headache. And if all went according to plan, she would be far from the Mediran palace.

"Well, gooood," he said, stumbling suddenly. "Briar root, right? How ... did ... you ... ?"

"The ring on my hand," she said. "It's laced with briar root." She blinked. Why had she said that? She never revealed that kind of information, not to him of all people. She never gave away her secrets.

He laughed suddenly, too loudly. "Well, you've got briar root too. It's . . . in . . . the knife handle."

Cassandra blinked again, her vision suddenly swimming. Briar root. In the knife. He had known she would go for the knife. Frustration surged in her gut, tinged with a grudging admiration. Why could she never get the best of him?

She was so sleepy. It had been ages since she'd last slept, she was sure of it. She could take a little nap now, right? Just briefly. Arphaxad would sleep too. Then she could bring him to the rendezvous point and take the Mediran king's greatest asset back to Rendra. That had been part of the plan, surely? Had she been supposed to see him at all? Or had there been something else she was supposed to get for the queen? She couldn't remember anymore.

She slumped to the ground, her head suddenly pounding. It took her a moment to realize that Arphaxad was on the ground beside her too.

Damn.

"I think . . . we can call this . . . a draw," she heard him say. His voice sounded distant, so far away.

"Is there ever . . . a draw . . . in what we do?" she managed around her thickening tongue.

"No," he said. "But somehow . . . you're the only one . . . I can't get the best of."

She might have laughed at that if she weren't so tired.

Her world swam and then went black.

Chapter 2

"That was incredibly, stupidly reckless."

There was frost in the Rendran queen's voice. Cassandra kept her eyes on the obsidian and quartz patterning the floor of the throne room, a sour mixture of shame and frustration tinging the back of her throat.

"Think what would have happened if you had been captured," the queen continued, her tone clipped and regal. "The queen's shadow tossed in a Mediran prison. How would that have looked to the Alliance? To Ineti? Or to any of the other powers on our border?"

Cassandra fought the urge to snap out a retort in her defense. She had been somewhat reckless, sure, but she'd had a plan. And she hadn't been captured in the end. It had all just ended . . . stupidly.

When she'd been late to the rendezvous point, Tomas, the captain of the queen's guard who had been her second on the mission, had come to find her. He'd said she'd been slumped near the road outside the palace, stripped of her weapons. Annoyance had slid through her. Outside the palace. Not in it.

And *he* had been nowhere to be seen.

Cassandra had seethed the entire way back to Rendra. He had let her go. But why? Was this just another part of his game? Another thing he could use to laugh at her?

"You may rise, shadow," the queen said.

Cassandra straightened from the deep curtsy she'd been holding. The queen's face was a mask of sternness and propriety. Her dark, graying hair was swept back from her cheeks, giving her face a heightened, regal angularity. She was seated in a tall throne made of woven metal and inlaid with lapis lazuli that had been the seat of the kings and queens of Rendra for hundreds of years. Her gown of deep blue was fastened with tiny gold buttons to the neck, and Cassandra could see lines around her mouth that hadn't been there even a few months before.

The queen had been young when she'd ascended the throne eighteen years prior—hardly twenty-seven, not much older than Cassandra was now. She was the only legitimate child of the prior king, and she had never married, though there had been more than one ambitious courtier who would have jumped at the chance.

"Now," the queen said, casting a look at Tomas who stood at attention not far behind Cassandra. "Thank you for doing your duty, captain, and keeping my shadow safe."

Cassandra did her best to keep her fists from clenching. Here, in the throne room, even with just Tomas and a few of the queen's other advisors watching, was not the place to break decorum.

"I expect a full, written report by morning," the queen continued, addressing Tomas. "You are dismissed."

"Your Highness," Tomas said with a quick bow. He gave Cassandra a nod—of pity or solidarity, she wasn't sure—then turned and left the hall.

Silence fell over the grand space, and Cassandra's eyes wandered up to the ornately carved marble that arched above the queen. When used for holding court or greeting foreign dignitaries, the room came alive with movement and color and life—but now, in the emptiness, it felt a bit too much like a tomb.

Cassandra did her best to keep a neutral smile as the queen rose. Her advisors, dressed in the heavy ceremonial garb of the court, rose as well. Cassandra felt suddenly small beneath their gazes.

"You must be tired," the queen said at last. "Retire to your chamber for the night. I will speak with you in the morning."

"Yes, Your Highness."

Cassandra's chest tightened, and she did her best to keep her frustration from showing. The queen hadn't even offered her a chance to defend herself before Tomas. Before the advisors.

Her mind flashed suddenly to a silver fox mask and the sting of a knife at her back. For a moment, her heartbeat quickened. She could not think about him now. She was already embarrassed enough.

Cassandra swept another grand curtsy and turned to go.

"Shadow?" the queen said.

Cassandra paused, her eyes focused on the open door of paneled cedar at the end of the hall.

"I have never known you to act without thought. Do not do something so rash again. For my sake."

Cassandra gave a quick nod of deference and left the hall.

***

The queen was lounging on an ornate divan by the window when Cassandra entered the royal suite. The older woman turned as Cassandra pushed the tall bookshelf closed with a click and batted a cobweb from above her eye. The narrow corridor into the royal suite had been built as a means of escape many, many years ago. There were few who knew of its existence—but the queen's shadow, as the face of the royal intelligence network, was one of them.

"You know, when I cast you in the role of shadow, it was supposed to be a purely ceremonial position," the queen said as Cassandra dropped into a tall chair with elegantly embroidered cushions.

Cassandra raised a brow at the queen. "You can hardly have expected me to keep it ceremonial, *Your Highness*. Besides, Andre clearly didn't intend for it to be."

The queen sighed, but Cassandra detected a hint of amusement in it. "I do appreciate your efforts for my sake, Cassandra. But what you tried with Ilin Serra—what I said in the throne room was true. It was reckless."

Cassandra's nostrils flared at the mention of his name. "It wasn't reckless, Elena. I swear. Nothing is ever straightforward with him. It's like an elaborate dance. A game. I know what I'm doing."

"Do you?" The queen arched an elegant brow. "It seems to me that if you refused to play at all, you might come out ahead."

"I play by my rules, not his," Cassandra said tightly. "You shouldn't worry so much. I know what I'm doing."

"You're my *sister*, Cassandra." The queen leaned forward earnestly. "My only sister. It's my duty to worry."

"Half-sister," Cassandra muttered.

"That doesn't make a difference!" the queen snapped. "Certainly not to Medira and certainly not to me."

"Medira doesn't know who I am," Cassandra returned, the old anger flaring in her chest. "The court *here* doesn't even know who I am." Because her father—and Elena's—had never claimed her publicly. There was almost a twenty-year age gap between them. It would have been a scandal. And there were always those who might try to use her to depose her sister, though being queen of Rendra was the last thing in the world Cassandra wanted.

The queen nodded. "And I have gone to great pains to keep it that way, for your own safety. And to protect your position as shadow. Which was something *you* wanted, by the way. So, when you do something like this . . . " She trailed off.

Cassandra knew she was right. It was imperative that no one knew of her true relationship to the queen. She would lose her freedom in an instant. And Cassandra didn't think she could stand to live cooped up in the palace the way the queen did.

"Well," Cassandra said into the silence. "I did achieve my goal at least."

The queen's head snapped up. "You did?"

"Of course," Cassandra replied a little too vehemently. She'd let herself get distracted, sure, but she'd still done her duty. "Well, mostly."

"Oh no." The queen swung her legs off the divan and fixed Cassandra with an exasperated stare.

Cassandra forced an overly bright smile. "I did manage to find my way into the quarters of the Inetian ambassador to Medira."

The queen nodded. It had been the true purpose of the mission. Her game with Ilin Serra had been a stupid distraction.

"I uncovered correspondence from the Inetian emperor to the ambassador. It confirmed that the rumors are true—that Medira does intend a marriage alliance." Cassandra suppressed a shudder. The Mediran king was well on his way to sixty, and the Inetian princess was barely nineteen.

The queen sounded suddenly tired when she finally did speak. "And what is the intention of this alliance?"

Cassandra opened her mouth and then shut it again. She still wasn't sure why a nation as powerful as Ineti would want to ally itself with a state as small as Medira. Rendra and Medira inhabited the same peninsula south across the sea from Ineti—but the two nations were fairly insular, with little in the way of resources Ineti did not already have access to from their own lands. It simply didn't make any sense.

"I'm still not sure," Cassandra admitted.

The queen sighed, and for a moment, Cassandra could see through her mask to the worry beneath. Even in private, she maintained a facade. A facade Cassandra had rarely been able to break through.

"I discovered something else too," Cassandra continued. She could still see the sharp lines of the pen strokes across the paper, smudged in places where ink had blotted out of the pen. "There was another letter—an anonymous letter—that mentioned something about an Inetian presence in the Malathi pass."

"The Malathi pass?" the queen said, leaning forward. The pass sat in the remote southern mountains that passed through both Rendra and Medira, though the pass itself was firmly inside Mediran borders.

Cassandra nodded. "These Inetians plan to meet with the enclave of Sorothi chanters there."

The queen's brows knit together. "But why? What could they want with the chanters?"

They had all heard stories of the Sorothi chanters, of the power they wielded—power that tore at the fabric of the world when it was used. Power that could open a gateway to a realm of shadow and release the monsters hiding within—monsters that had no business in their world.

The chanters' magic had been banned by the Alliance to the south, Ineti to the north, and most other states within Rendra's orbit, and so they'd retreated to more remote areas to continue their work. They'd settled in the Malathi pass in the south-west of Medira, not far from the Rendran border, twenty years earlier. They'd kept mostly to themselves, so Medira had left them alone. If Ineti wanted access to the chanters, then there was something very, very wrong going on.

"I don't know," Cassandra said, trying to keep her frustration at bay. She wished she had more to tell the queen. She had rifled through as much of the correspondence as she dared before snatching the letter and slinking away along the eaves of the palace where the court was celebrating the solstice. That had been when she'd spotted *him*. And she hadn't been able to resist the thought of messing with him.

"So, this letter," the queen said. "Do you have it?"

Cassandra's face flamed. "I did have it," she muttered, dropping her eyes from the queen's.

The queen watched her for a moment. "Ah," she said at last. "Ilin Serra took it."

Cassandra nodded. Damn that man. "That's why I need to go to the pass. We need to figure out what Ineti wants with the chanters. Why they are looking for an alliance with Medira. All I know is that this cannot be good for Rendra." She also knew that *he* would act on the contents of the letter immediately, now that he knew she'd read it. And she had to act fast before he did anything to thwart her.

The queen sighed, passing a tired hand over her face. "Yes. Someone must go. But it does not have to be you." She paused. "Send Isabel. That girl has shown a lot of promise."

Cassandra's fists clenched. She couldn't deny that Isabel was the best agent in her network, but she needed her here. "It has to be me, Elena," she said vehemently. "Isabel is promising, but I'm the best you have. And I know Ilin Serra better than anyone. I can spot his tricks from miles away."

The queen raised her brows. "Can you?"

Cassandra's cheeks flamed again. "Yes," she said stubbornly.

The queen hesitated. "It's quite a journey to get to the pass."

"I have my ways," Cassandra returned. "You know I do. Contacts along the route. I am the queen's shadow, after all. I inherited the knowledge of those who came before me."

The queen sighed, tapping a finger against the lace of her gown. "I know," she said at last. "I know you're right. But I worry that Ilin Serra has this knowledge too." She paused. "You are quite blind when it comes to him."

"I am not!" Cassandra snapped. "And if he has this knowledge, then maybe Medira will rethink their alliance with Ineti. I need to move quickly, to get there before Ilin Serra does. To understand what Ineti wants."

The queen stood and made her way to the window. The Rendran capital spread out below, its old stone buildings glistening in the afternoon light. Her sister was worried about her, but Cassandra had always shown herself to have a level head before. She knew she was the one person the queen trusted beyond all others. There were too many political games that went on at court.

"All right," the queen conceded at last. "You leave at dawn. Outfit yourself accordingly. It won't be an easy journey."

Cassandra nodded. She had been out to the Malathi pass once before to make contact with those who had been allied to Andre Alarcon, the shadow before her. To make sure they were still willing to serve. She had people who could guide her.

"I won't be reckless, Elena," she said.

"I certainly hope so." The queen sighed. "Just don't let Ilin Serra get to your head again."

"I won't," Cassandra said. "I swear it."

Chapter 3

The cart rumbled along the rutted mountain road, its wheels groaning with each rotation. Cassandra did her best to keep her teeth from rattling from her perch in the back, gripping the rough sides of the cart for dear life.

Her bow rested on her lap, and her pack and a quiver of arrows sat beside her. She ran her fingers over the smooth wood of her bow, as familiar as if it were an extension of her body. The symbol of the queen's shadow, and a gift from her sister.

She had been eight years old when the queen had first come to see her. It was hardly a month after the queen's coronation, and Cassandra had been awed by the tall, terrifying woman dressed in the regal black of mourning. The queen had come quietly into the house where Cassandra lived with her grandmother on the outskirts of the Rendran capital. There had been no fanfare, no pageantry, no great carriage pulled by eight white horses. No one beyond the queen and a tall, familiar-looking man with graying hair, twinkling eyes, and a curved bow of rowan slung across his back.

"Your Highness," Cassandra's grandmother had gasped, immediately dropping into a deep curtsy and elbowing Cassandra to do the same. Cassandra had done so reluctantly and awkwardly, and only because there had been so much urgency in her grandmother's tone.

"To what do we owe the pleasure of the sovereign's visit?" her grandmother had continued with more deference than Cassandra had ever heard from the old woman.

"I have come to see . . . to see Cassandra," the queen had said.

Cassandra's head had snapped up then, and she'd met the queen's gaze before she'd realized what she was doing. The queen's brown eyes had twinkled, chasing away some of the sadness that lingered there.

"But why?" she'd said before she could stop herself.

"Because" the queen said, "I want to meet my sister."

Cassandra had learned many things that day. She'd learned that her mother had worked at the palace for a time, and when Cassandra was born, the king had set them up in the house in which Cassandra now lived with her grandmother. When her mother had died of a wasting illness a few years later, Cassandra's grandmother had moved from the small village a three days' journey from the capital to take care of her.

And she had a sister. A sister who'd had no knowledge of Cassandra's existence until their father's death. No knowledge that she wasn't the only child of the king until Andre—the tall, familiar-looking man—had told her. As the king's shadow, he'd known all the king's secrets. And as the king's shadow, he'd been watching Cassandra for a long time. The new queen needed a shadow of her own. So, Andre had taken Cassandra on as his apprentice, and she had excelled. The queen had intended for the position to be ceremonial, but Andre never had.

Cassandra's heart twisted at the thought of the man who had become a father figure to her. But he was gone now too, taken a few years earlier by an illness that had turned him into a shell of his former self.

"Road ends here," the driver called from the front of the cart. He pulled on the reins and the cart rumbled to a stop.

Cassandra grabbed her pack, her quiver, and her bow before hopping out and tossing the man a small bag that clinked with coin. He gave her a nod before tugging his donkey's reins and turning the cart back around. She waited until the cart disappeared into the trees before starting up the slope and toward the pass.

The high summer sun beamed over the mountains, bathing the forest in shades of green and gold. Far above, she could see birds hopping between branches in the thick canopy of pines. She pulled her gray cloak closer around her shoulders. Even in summer, the air here was cool and crisp—so different from the arid warmth she was used to in the Rendran capital.

The road narrowed ahead, turning into a single-lane footpath that sloped sharply upward and disappeared into the trees. A stream trickled somewhere in the distance, likely fed by the snowmelt of the higher peaks beyond the pass.

The queen had been right. It was a long journey to Malathi pass. But she had made it in little more than a week—in time, she hoped, to intercept the Inetian caravan.

But that was the strange thing. Cassandra had reached out to her contacts to see what the whispers were about the pass—but there had been very little in the way of information. There had been no mention of a caravan leaving Ineti and traveling toward Medira—not anywhere. Surely a group of Inetians traveling through the peninsula couldn't remain undetected for long. Could it?

The path turned rockier as Cassandra climbed, and she was thankful when she finally topped the rise and peered down into the Malathi pass.

Deep greens and sharp grays blended in the valley, pierced by the shadows cast by the midday sun. Cassandra knew from discrete meetings with her contacts that the enclave lay about a mile along the valley from this road, nestled against the mountain. She checked her direction with the sun before setting off westward along the ridge, stray branches from the undergrowth nipping at her clothes.

It wasn't long before she smelled the smoke of cookfires. The enclave.

A dozen timber-hewn cottages with thatched roofs dotted the floor of the valley, their parchment windows glowing faintly with the orange light of enchanted orb fire. A few humanoid shapes moved around the makeshift village, dressed in the nondescript gray robes Cassandra knew the chanters favored, hanging up washing, cooking, and corralling the gaggle of children who dashed barefoot between the houses. Pens holding pigs, goats, and chickens adjoined some of the cabins, and there were a few donkeys and oxen for pulling carts.

A wide, flat cookfire glowing with embers lay in the center of the village, where a few figures lingered, and

Cassandra thought she could detect the peaty smell of pipe smoke wafting through the air.

There was no sign of an Inetian caravan.

A worn path ran back from the village toward the mountain, where Cassandra could see a jagged opening gashed into the rock. Two orbs of enchanted fire marked the entrance. A cave. The first sign that this wasn't an ordinary settlement.

She slunk farther along the ridge line, careful to keep enough distance that even if someone happened to look up, they wouldn't be able to see her. A woman in a gray robe made her way into the cave entrance. A small child came out and scampered into one of the thatch-roof huts.

Cassandra was deciding whether to move closer or wait until nightfall to gain access to the cave when three men emerged. One was dressed in the gray of the chanter enclave, his hair a shock of white, his skin almost translucently pale, like the people of the Alliance in the south. But the other two were not, their skin and hair showing a deep brown beside the much paler chanter. Cassandra took a quick breath and moved closer to listen.

"We were told we would see results sooner than this," one of the men was saying to the chanter. He was tall and broad with bronze skin and thick black hair, and Cassandra could make out a scar that ran from his jaw down beneath his tunic. His accent was unmistakably Inetian.

The chanter shook his head. "You were not promised anything beyond access to our knowledge. The rate at which your men learn is beyond my power to control. And besides, we haven't seen anything of which we were promised in—"

"His eminence does not break his promises!" the Inetian cut in.

His eminence? Cassandra's brows drew together. The Inetian emperor was always addressed as His Majesty.

"He better not," the chanter said, and Cassandra could feel a pulse of power crackle in the air. The Inetian took a wary step back. "I don't allow people who don't keep their promises to live."

Cassandra's brows drew together. What promises? Were the chanters teaching the Inetians their magic? That was a wholly terrifying thought on its own, but what could the Inetians have possibly promised in return to reach that kind of agreement?

A twig snapped in the bracken to her right, and she froze. The tread had been too heavy, too broad, to be a hare or a mountain goat. She reached for the knife at her belt, her heart thundering in her throat, and waited for the sound to come again.

There was another snap, and this time, Cassandra could make out a figure in the trees draped in a nondescript black cloak. The figure was hardly three meters from her. He peered over the ridge for a moment, just as Cassandra had, then stepped back, turned his head, and looked directly at her.

Cassandra moved before the figure could. In one swift motion, she kicked for his knees and dropped him. The figure grunted as he crashed to the ground—a clearly masculine sound—and Cassandra was on him in an instant. He grunted again as she shoved her knee in his kidney and pressed her knife roughly against his throat.

The figure stilled, and for a moment, all Cassandra could hear was the sound of their breathing in the stillness of the afternoon.

A beat passed as her eyes struggled to focus on his face, and then the figure chuckled—a low, melodious sound—and an all too familiar voice breathed against her cheek, "Why, Cass. I missed you too."

Heat flooded her body in a tidal wave. Arphaxad Ilin Serra lay on the forest floor beneath her, his dark eyes twinkling up at her with maddening amusement. And her knife was pressed to his throat.

"You!" she sputtered before she could stop herself. "What are you doing here?"

His grin widened. "I have you to thank for my presence here. If you hadn't found that letter for me—"

She pressed the knife more sharply against his throat, and he hissed. She leaned in and gave him her sweetest smile. "It might be prudent for you to remember that I'm the one with the knife to your throat."

Arphaxad grunted, and she thought she could feel him tense, as if ready to spring. She shoved her knee into his kidney again, and he grunted but lay back.

"You're in rare form today," he wheezed. That damn glint of arrogance was still in his eyes. As if he knew something she didn't.

"I'll ask you again," she said softly. "What are you doing here?"

His mouth curved in that all-too-familiar grin. "I wager it's the same thing you are." He paused, as if shoring himself for what he was about to say. "And if you let me up, I'll tell you about it."

She almost laughed out loud. Let him up? He had to be kidding. "Oh, sure. I'm just supposed to trust you." He was the one she could never get the best of. The one who always managed to slip through her fingers. She was not about to allow that to happen again. Not when she had him here, beneath her, at knife point.

Even if they were in his territory, miles from the Rendran capital. It would take an impossible act of will for her to get him back to the queen in one piece, without allowing him to escape. She supposed she could subdue him long enough to slip his grasp. But then there was the Inetian presence in the chanter enclave to worry about. And she needed more information. Frustration rose in her gut. This was starting to feel all too familiar—they had been here too many times before, and every time, he'd taken something from her.

He didn't break her gaze. "Look at it as a trade of sorts, Cass. I'm as in the dark as you are about this. And if Ineti wants something to do with the Sorothi chanters and their earth magic—well, it's not a good sign for either Rendra or Medira." He paused and shifted beneath her again. He was warm where their bodies made contact, and suddenly she was sharply aware of everywhere his body pressed against hers. A strange shiver zipped through her.

It had been a long time since he'd been stupid enough to let her knock him down like this. Not since five years ago, when she'd stumbled on the elusive Mediran agent Andre hadn't been able to pin down for the last few years of his career. He'd been slipping along the roof of the Rendran palace, dressed, not as innocuously as he seemed to think, as a footman. She'd gotten close enough to get a good look at his face, to take in his annoyingly handsome jaw and aquiline nose, his olive skin tanned from time spent in the sparring yard, and then he had promptly slipped her grasp.

Annoyance at the memory, at him, at herself, flared through her now, and she kneed him in the kidney again, then got to her feet, careful to keep the knife at his throat. She was not going to allow him to slip away again.

Arphaxad grunted, then scrambled into a sitting position. His hair was longer than when she had last seen him, curling around his ears, and there was a dark line of stubble at his jaw. His tunic was black and well-fitting, devoid of any mark that might tie him to his king.

For a moment as they watched each other in the midafternoon sun, he looked haggard, tired in a way she had never seen him before. But a moment later, that smirk was back, his annoyingly impenetrable mask slamming back down in place.

"Talk," Cassandra said.

His gaze narrowed. "As you know, Medira has an . . . *interest* . . . in what Ineti is doing in our lands."

An interest. Cassandra almost snorted. "The marriage to the Inetian emperor's daughter. I've heard."

Arphaxad's gaze skittered from hers for a moment, then snapped back. "I suppose I would have lost respect for you if you hadn't known about that."

Her lips curved. "Glad I'm not a disappointment."

"You never disappoint me, Cass," he said.

Warmth pooled in her belly. The queen's words came back to her in a rush. "You are quite blind when it comes to him. Don't do anything rash." Her hand tightened on the dagger. Her sister was wrong. She was not blind when it came to him. He was arrogant, sly, and not to be underestimated. There wasn't anything to be blind about.

"What do you know about Ineti's presence here then?" she asked. "I'd expect the king's nephew to have some insight."

Arphaxad gave a dry chuckle. "You would think that, wouldn't you? But as I said before, I know just about as much as you." He paused, eyeing her for a moment, as if weighing his next words. "I think we can help each other."

Help each other? Her brows shot up. They had never once been on the same side. That was just not what they did.

"Work together," she repeated dumbly. "With you."

"Oh, come now, Cass," he said, his mouth quirking. "I'm not so bad."

She couldn't keep from snorting this time. "So, I'm to help Medira secure an alliance with Ineti? That doesn't sound like something I'd be interested in, *Phax*."

He spread his hands. "On the contrary, I think it would be mutually beneficial. With the entire hoard of Sorothi chanters down there who wield who knows what kind of magic as well as unknown Inetian caravanners, we could both use a little back up." He paused. "Besides. I have . . . doubts . . . that whatever we uncover will lead to Medira following through with this alliance."

Cassandra's eyebrows rose further. "So, you want my help to . . . end the alliance with Incti?"

"Which can only be a good thing for Rendra."

She couldn't argue with that logic. They both wanted to understand what was happening in that valley. And if he thought it was something that could break Medira's pending marriage alliance with Ineti, then it had to be serious.

"I still have no reason to trust you."

He met her gaze for a long moment. "You don't. And I have no reason to trust you. It's a choice."

Her heart gave a sudden thud. A choice. She had allowed him to get the best of her too many times. But there *was* truth to what he was saying.

And there was a part of her that really, really wanted to play the game he was asking her to play.

"Besides," he said, "you know that if it weren't for you, I wouldn't be here at all."

Her cheeks flamed. If she hadn't been so stupid back in Medira and let him get his hands on that letter . . . "Is that a thank you I hear?" she said, pushing back her embarrassment.

A muscle twitched in his jaw. She almost burst into a surprised laugh. For once, Arphaxad Ilin Serra had not known about something going on in his own kingdom. That delighted her far more than it should.

She grinned at him. "Well, then," she said sweetly. "It seems you do have me to thank for this."

He arched a brow at her, and her grin widened.

"It's only polite to offer some sort of thanks for a favor, I believe."

"Is it?" he said, leaning forward so that his neck brushed the edge of her knife. Their gazes locked. She would not be the first to look away.

An earth-shattering boom rocked the valley below. Cassandra was tossed away from the ridge like a rag doll, her knife flying from her hands and skittering away into the forest. Her shoulder slammed against a fallen trunk as the world turned white, and the breath was knocked from her lungs.

For a moment, she lay still, trying to get her bearings, to figure out what had just happened. Arphaxad. She scrambled to her feet, swiftly drawing another knife from her boot.

He was crumpled on the ground a hundred feet away. He grunted and stiffly pulled himself to his feet, and they were left staring at each other across the forest, a cacophony of birds scattering into the air above them. A strange white glow radiated from the valley, along with a cloying sense of wrongness that was impossible to describe.

Cassandra swallowed, her eyes wide. "What in the name of the Archer was that?"

Arphaxad's usually composed face was ashen, his mouth pressed together in a thin line. "That was the sound of magic gone awry."

Chapter 4

Cassandra peered down the ridge at the valley below. It looked much the same as it had before the explosion. Before *he'd* shown up. Her mouth twisted.

Arphaxad crouched beside her in the brush, and she did her best to ignore his presence.

The inviting glow of the enchanted orb fire at the mouth of the cave was gone, disintegrated by the explosion. Gray silt still hung suspended in the air, obscuring the cave entrance almost entirely from view. It was just as well. She found it incredibly hard to look at—as if something had shifted about the earth below, something vast and inexplicable and *wrong*.

People had emerged from their houses, gathering in packs and talking in harsh whispers as they stared in horror at the inky blackness of the cave mouth.

"Idiots!" one of the chanters growled as he ran toward the cave. His graying hair was long and tied in a tail at the nape of his neck. "We should never have agreed to this. They're going to destroy us all!"

A few other chanters peeled off from their respective groups and followed him, their faces grim and drawn. Men were stumbling out of the cave now, their robes and tunics crumpled and streaked with dust. One of the men hung limply between two others as they dragged him into the open air, and Cassandra could see blood encrusted in his dark hair. Another man clutched at his arm, wincing with every step he took.

"It was Akil," one of the men gasped. He was young, younger than Cassandra even, with curling dark hair and a slim build. "He—his chant slipped. He's gone." He leaned over and vomited.

"Damn novices," one of the chanters muttered.

Horror washed over her in a nauseating wave. Arphaxad had said that the explosion had been caused by magic. Were the chanters teaching the Inetians? She had caught wind of their conversation earlier, but she hadn't wanted to believe it. It couldn't be. Surely the emperor, as ruthless as he was, wouldn't condone something like this?

The white-haired chanter emerged from the cave a moment later, his mouth drawn in a grim line.

"Gustav!" the graying chanter snapped. "We told you this would happen, but you made the Archer-forsaken deal anyway!"

"I don't have time for this, Victor," the white-haired chanter—Gustav—said evenly. "We need everyone with the strength to create a circle in the cavern, now."

Victor opened his mouth as if he were going to say something more, but the woman beside him laid a hand on his arm, and he snapped it shut.

"*Now*, Victor," Gustav said, his voice taking on a tone of danger.

"We're all going to pay for your folly," Victor muttered. He pushed bodily past Gustav, his shoulder knocking against the shorter man's, and was swallowed up by the silty haze.

Cassandra glanced over at Arphaxad. He was poised like a cat, worry gathering in his jaw. This whole situation had been unimaginable only a few hours ago. But now here she was, working with the man she had sworn to keep one step ahead of, trying to contain a threat that might bring about the end of both their kingdoms. If the Inetians wanted the chanters' power for themselves—she shuddered.

The group of chanters was disappearing into the lingering smoke at the mouth of the cave now, but no one rushed forward to help the staggering men.

"Are they going in there to . . . fix whatever it was that happened?" Cassandra asked in a whisper.

"I don't know," Arphaxad breathed beside her.

"We're going to have to go in there." She took a step along the ridge, then froze as his fingers closed around her wrist.

"Wait," he said. She tensed, ready to throw his grasp—and break his arm—if she had to. He let go and retreated a few steps.

"Wait," he said again.

"For what?" she snapped. She wasn't used to working with other people—let alone with *him*. And if he insisted on slowing her down, then this—whatever *this* was—wouldn't last for very long.

"Let them get farther in. We don't want to risk getting caught. The passageway looks narrow. If we run across anyone . . . it won't go well for us."

She sighed. "It might be better if I went in alone. I'm smaller than you are. There are more crevices in which I can hide."

He sorted. "You're insane if you think I'm going to let you go in there alone."

Her mouth quirked. Of course he wouldn't. Neither of them could risk losing sight of the other. Even with whatever strange sort of peace lay between them.

"Fine, then," she said. "But don't get left behind."

They crept along the top of the ridge, careful to keep out of sight of the villagers below.

"So, you trust me now?" he whispered. His voice was low but still dripped with that maddening arrogance.

"Absolutely not," she returned. "But you haven't tried to kill me yet, so that's something."

Arphaxad snorted. "I've had plenty of chances to kill you before, Cass."

She bit back the "ha" that rose in her throat. She'd had plenty of chances to kill him before too. But she hadn't.

The group of chanters that had gathered at the opening had disappeared inside, and the haggard, wide-eyed men who had stumbled out had made their way to the other side of the enclave, as if they wanted to get as far away from whatever they had witnessed as possible.

"There," Arphaxad said, his voice hardly above a whisper. She followed his finger to the boulder perched just outside the cave entrance. It was large and flat, wide enough to hide them both.

"I see it," she said, as way of confirmation.

She followed him down the ridge, acutely aware of his presence ahead of her. He moved carefully, quietly, hardly making a sound in the stillness of the woods.

He reached the boulder before she did, and she dropped into the space beside him. The crushed, blackened shells of the enchanted orb fire lay scattered by the cave. Dust coated her tongue, sulfurous and cloying, and she pulled the edge of her cloak over her nose to help her breathe. The strange white glow that had hung over the valley after the explosion had faded. Cassandra shuddered. She had entered a lot of unsavory spaces in her time as shadow, but this . . . something about this seemed much, much worse.

Arphaxad slipped around the bolder and dropped into the cave entrance. She followed half a beat later.

It was dark inside, and the entrance narrowed as they moved swiftly along, the damp stone ceiling dropping until it was only a few inches above Arphaxad's head. There wasn't time to feel their way slowly. They needed to get in, find the information they were looking for, and get out.

The sense of wrongness intensified with every step, pressing against her temples until her head felt like it would crack apart. For a moment, it was hard to breathe, and she forced herself to take slow, steady breaths, just like Andre had taught her.

"I chose you for a reason," her mentor had told her. "And not just because you are the queen's sister. You have a level head on your shoulders and a fighter's spirit. Those are things that can't be taught."

The orange glow of orb fire flickered like a pinprick in the distance, casting distorted shadows up against the rock. Something crinkled beneath Cassandra's boot. She froze, then leaned down to pick it up. A letter, crumpled and boot-marked, with a blank wax seal. She shoved it into her belt.

A moment later, a dark alcove dredged into the rock to their left, and Cassandra caught sight of a flat makeshift writing desk. Paper had been blown every which way—probably from the explosion—and was likely why the letter had flown out into the hallway. She ducked to pick up a few more of the scattered pages. She jumped when she realized how far ahead Arphaxad was, then hurried after him. She had to pull up sharply when she almost slammed into his back.

"Shh," he said.

Voices echoed from somewhere ahead—a mix of men and women—but it didn't sound like the standard hum of chatter. The voices moved together in a grotesque, pounding rhythm, the words a mash of sounds, intoned, but moving together as one. A chant.

Cassandra swallowed. Andre may have spent years preparing her to take on the role of queen's shadow, but she wasn't sure even he could have prepared her for the wrongness of *this*.

Arphaxad signaled for them to begin moving again toward the glow and the rising sound of voices. They rounded the final corner and found themselves looking out into a cavern. The path dropped suddenly away, and a narrow wooden staircase tapered down the rock deeper into the massive cavern.

Toward the back, a group of chanters stood in a tight circle, their hands joined as they swayed together in the rhythm of their speech. She could see the pale, white-haired chanter among them, as well as the man who had expressed his disgust for the Inetians. Power crackled in the cavern, a force she couldn't see but that she could feel pressing deep into her bones.

Horror swirled in the pit of her stomach. There, behind the swaying chanters, was *something*—a rift, a tear, a distortion, that hung grossly in the air. It was a jagged black gash that pulsed a few feet above the cave floor, a twisted, sucking, vile thing.

She had heard the stories of the monsters that lived in the realm of shadow, a domain of darkness beyond the physical world, one that could only be accessed by magic so powerful it tore apart the fabric of reality. There the shadows fed on the living, and if a rift were fully opened, they could break through with the power to destroy the world.

The rift pulsed, as if trying to tear itself open wider, expanding its reach. The chant rose and swelled, beating back at the crackling darkness.

Arphaxad had called it magic gone awry. Cassandra thought that had been a gross understatement.

Something moved in the cave to the left of the chanters. A thin line of light erupted in the darkness, then slowly widened until it was more than five feet across. Cassandra's heart beat wildly as, a moment later, one man and then another, both dressed in the gray robes of chanters, appeared as if from nowhere. Cassandra could see the faded outline of the rocks of the cave behind the ripple of light. A moment later, the light drew back together and disappeared with a snap.

Around the cavern, more men appeared, and it was then that Cassandra noticed the doors—twelve in all—that pulsed between filamented forged-metal frames set into the rock, portals to elsewhere. They stood at equidistant intervals around the space, one sitting hardly fifty feet behind the garish rift, its metal frame already warped—but the door still flickered with life.

The rift crackled again at the increase in power as the new chanters joined the circle, and a wave of nausea at the strangeness of the magic rolled over her, hot and fast. They needed to get out of here, now.

She tugged on Arphaxad's sleeve. He turned, and she could see that his face was as ashen as hers had to be. He gave her a quick nod, and they turned and fled the cave.

They burst out into a cool, radiant afternoon. Cassandra didn't stop moving until they had darted past the boulder and clambered back up the ridge. She didn't stop until her foot snagged on a root and she almost went down.

She caught herself, then whirled to face Arphaxad under the trees. The sun was no longer directly overhead, and the forest was flooded with a deep orange glow.

"What *was* that?" she said.

Arphaxad was breathing as heavily as she was, and his usually composed features were ashen. "It's a rift. A tear in the fabric of the world. It's what happens when magic gets out of control and . . . and consumes the user. Whoever that unlucky Akil was . . . it looks like he's gone."

"Inside that thing?" Cassandra said, trying her best to keep her voice even.

Arphaxad nodded, his face grim. "Trapped forever. A fate worse than death."

Cassandra waved her arm in his direction. "How do you know all this?"

Arphaxad shook his head. "It's my job to know what's going on in Medira. The enclave has always been part of that." He frowned. "Except this . . . this is very, very bad."

"I can see that," Cassandra snapped. "What about the other chanters? That white light. The—the metal frames around the room. It was like they appeared from nowhere."

Arphaxad hesitated.

"We're in this together now, Phax," she said, her voice low. "I need to know. It looks like this isn't just about just Medira and Rendra anymore."

He glanced back toward the valley. "It's their magic. That's . . . how it works. They can open doors between two places and walk through, as if distance doesn't exist."

Cassandra stared at him, trying to comprehend what he had just said. So that was the dangerous earth magic the Sorothi chanters dabbled in. A power that could make whatever nation wielded it too strong for any other nation to match.

"But that's . . . that's impossible."

"Obviously not," he drawled, the arrogance back in his voice. "It's dangerous though. Too dangerous, as you can see. If the chanters hadn't been there to beat the rift back . . . well, it could consume this entire valley. And who knows if it would stop there."

"So that's why their magic is outlawed," Cassandra whispered.

Arphaxad nodded. "Yes. But the Sorothi chanters believe it's a magic worth pursuing on their own terms. And so far, none of them have gone out of their way to abuse it."

"Until now," Cassandra said.

"Until now," he agreed.

They stood in silence for a moment, watching each other in the afternoon light. A light breeze picked up in the trees, rustling the leaves in an eerie hush. For the first time, Cassandra realized that there was no birdsong.

Arphaxad huffed out a breath. "I don't understand why, though. Why would the Inetian emperor take this kind of risk? Ineti has everything it could ever need—power, wealth, ships, men, weapons, food. Why send soldiers to learn something that's been outlawed for good reason?"

Cassandra shook her head. "I don't know that these men are acting at the behest of the emperor."

Arphaxad watched her for a moment. "Cass," he said slowly, "you took something, didn't you?"

Her mouth curved as she pulled the crumpled pages from beneath the band of her tunic. "What?" she said sweetly. "You mean this? It looked like a written in Inetian to me, so I . . . removed it."

Arphaxad's eyes glowed, and the corners of his mouth tipped up in an approving smile. "You really are delightful sometimes."

She snorted, pushing down the sudden warmth that rose in her chest. She glanced down at the letter and carefully unfolded it. She froze. There at the bottom of the page was a name signed in black ink: Sethos Amanakar. One of the sons of the emperor of Ineti.

Chapter 5

Thud. Arphaxad embedded a dagger in the side of a half-rotten tree stump. The hilt quivered in the waning light.

"How arrogant do you have to be to think that this . . . this ridiculous scheme will accomplish anything except war and bloodshed?" Arphaxad pulled another dagger from his belt and embedded it next to the first, his face blazing with rage. Cassandra had never seen him this worked up about anything before.

"It doesn't seem like he's thinking much at all," she said. Her brows rose as Arphaxad embedded a third knife in the stump, the blades nestled together in a neat triangle.

"Clearly." He kicked at a fallen branch in the detritus. It skittered across the undergrowth and shattered against a tree.

The rest of the correspondence Cassandra had removed from the cave had proved to be just as illuminating as the name signed on that first letter. Sethos Amanakar was planning to use the chanters, and the power he learned from them, to stage a coup against his father. And the Inetian ambassador to Medira was in league with him.

It wasn't exactly surprising that there was a plan to overthrow the Inetian emperor—Cassandra heard rumblings of that regularly. The Inetian emperor had fourteen children from a dizzying succession of queens and likely more illegitimate children as well. There was always someone who thought they could use one of his progenies to make a claim for the throne, especially in an empire that had been united by so much bloodshed and where there were generations of lingering tensions.

Amanakar was one of the lucky illegitimate sons to be claimed by the emperor when there were dozens more who never had been—and he was more well-connected than even some of his legitimate siblings from earlier queens who had fallen out of favor, since his mother was sister to one of the more well-connected, though now discarded queens.

Cassandra's mouth twisted at the thought. At least Amanakar had been claimed by his father when she'd just been discarded by hers. The old wound ached, more than she wanted to admit. She knew all too well how it felt to live in a world that claimed your birth was not valid, and she could understand some of what might drive Amanakar to want to overthrow a father who cared for little beyond getting pleasure and exerting power wherever and whenever he wanted.

It was a tale as old as time. Those in power always sought to use others to get what they wanted, no matter the consequences. She just wished Amanakar hadn't decided to go about it so stupidly.

That's what made *this* plan so much worse than the usual rumblings of uprising in Ineti: the gall of Amanakar to try to use magic that had been banned across the empire. Magic that could easily go awry and bring about the end of . . . a lot of things.

Frustration curled in her gut. It was her job to know about the changing power situation in and around Rendra, and she'd missed it. Amanakar had never come up as a threat before now—he'd always seemed to be a man simpering in the graces of the great emperor and leeching as much as he could get away with. While he wasn't threatening Rendra directly, he had sent men to the peninsula to learn from the Sorothi chanters. And that kind of power, and closeness, *was* a direct threat to Rendra. Especially if his aim was to throw the Inetian empire into chaos.

Arphaxad stared at the daggers in the stump, tension clear in every sinew of his body.

She understood his anger too. For him, this was more than just a small thing he hadn't been aware of. It was an enormous oversight, especially with the looming marriage alliance to the Inetian emperor's daughter. And if it hadn't been for Cassandra making an idiot of herself at the Mediran palace, he might not have known for weeks more.

Arphaxad pulled another knife and threw it at the stump. This one slipped past and skittered into the forest. He swore. She didn't like seeing him so on edge—he had a maddening ability to keep his composure, even under the tensest of circumstances, and for him to show his anger this openly showed how unsettling the situation was.

"What I want to know," Cassandra said as she picked up her bow and moved to stand beside him, "is why the enclave even agreed to help in the first place. They know the risks better than anyone. And they've spent their entire lives learning to control their magic. These Inetians clearly have not, judging by what we witnessed today."

Arphaxad sighed. "Something must be going on in the enclave. Something we don't know about."

He looked at her sidelong as she nocked an arrow and drew the string. The arrow thwacked into the stump right in the middle of the daggers. He made an appreciative noise. "Good shot."

"I'm imagining Amanakar's head," she said impishly.

He snorted, then drew another dagger and tossed it. It embedded in the stump just beside her arrow.

They were quiet for a moment, staring at the weapons in the fading light. The shadows had lengthened since they'd made their way back to the ridge, then deeper into the forest in hopes of avoiding prying eyes, of getting father away from the wrongness of the cave. It wouldn't be long before darkness fell. A tired ache was gathering in Cassandra's body, but she knew she couldn't think about rest anytime soon.

"What can Amanakar possibly offer the chanters?" she said finally. "Safety? The backing of a major power? All that seems like a gamble compared to what they have now in Medira."

Arphaxad nodded. The anger had drained from his face, and she could see the exhaustion that lay behind it.

She raised her bow again and sent another arrow thudding into the stump, sliding it between her first arrow and Arphaxad's dagger beside it.

"Now you're just showing off," he said. Cassandra's lips twitched, and she waited as he went to the stump and removed first his daggers and then her arrows.

"Amanakar's ploy is learning the secrets of the Sorothi chanters," he said as he returned, handing her the arrows. She watched carefully where he placed each dagger. Those were certainly not all the weapons he had on him, but it helped to know where some of them were. He arched a brow at her, and she gave him her sweetest smile.

"Possessing the ability to open a door to anywhere would certainly prove effective against your enemies," he continued.

Cassandra slipped the arrows back in her quiver. He was right. That kind of knowledge could give even a very small force an enormous upper hand. "Amanakar could open a door to his father's bedroom and kill him in his sleep and no one would ever know."

"Exactly." Arphaxad grimaced. "And if there's an influx of amateurs using this kind of power, how long do you think it will be before they start tearing rifts like we saw today? How long before something truly horrible comes slinking through?"

She quieted at his words. She never wanted to witness what she had this morning ever again. It had been so utterly wrong. Even here, up on the ridge and away from the cave, she could sense its pull, its wrongness, its distortion on the reality of their world.

"They'll destroy the world," she said soberly. "Or, at least, send the empire into chaos."

Arphaxad flexed his fingers, then pulled a dagger from his belt. She could sense his frustration again. "Bastard," he said.

Cassandra froze—that word. She hated that word. And coming from him, it somehow cut through her even more deeply.

He raised the dagger, readying it to throw. "He's going to get thousands killed, and all so he can get some sort of stupid, petty revenge on his father. The Inetian emperor is going to be sorry he ever claimed him."

The ground dropped out beneath Cassandra's feet. For a moment, she couldn't breathe. And then anger was coursing through her veins in a sudden, raging flood as the world came rushing back, and she couldn't stop herself from rounding on him. "Don't you dare say that!" Her nostrils flared. "You have absolutely no idea what it's like to have a father who doesn't want you!"

Arphaxad's gaze snapped to hers, his eyes widening briefly. That only made her angrier.

"You had a father who claimed you," she said, her voice rising. "You have no idea what it's like to be without a family for most of your life!"

She jerked away from him, yanking her bow into position. Damn it, damn it, damn it! She reached for an arrow, sending it hurtling toward the stump. Then another. And another.

Arphaxad was standing rigid now beside her. "I—" He took a step forward and then stopped.

"All I'm saying," she blundered on as she nocked another arrow, "is that I understand why a man like Sethos Amanakar might feel like he's owed something."

She sent another arrow into the stump. Her heart thundered wildly in her throat. What was wrong with her today? She should never have said anything. Would never have said it if he were anyone else. But she couldn't bear to have him think *that*.

Arphaxad was the first to break the silence. "Cass," he said softly. "You're right. You're absolutely right. I don't know what it's like."

She knew he didn't. He was the son of one of the king's brothers. He had loving parents, by all accounts, and a younger brother who adored him. He'd always had family.

Arphaxad swallowed. "But you do, Cass. I know. I know about who you are."

Her head snapped up, and she lowered her bow. "What?" Her world tilted again.

He slid the dagger he'd drawn back into its sheath. "I—it's my business to know these things. That you're the queen's sister."

The world seemed to spin around her, the darkening trees whirling faster and faster as her mind tried to catch up with what he had just said. He knew she was the queen's sister. He *knew*.

"Half-sister," she said before she could stop herself. She clenched her jaw, a cloying frustration spreading through her gut. If he hadn't been certain before, she'd beyond confirmed it for him now. "How?" she demanded. "How did you know?"

He shifted his weight, looking suddenly uncomfortable. "I—you look like her. And you came out of nowhere. Andre Alarcon took a seemingly random girl off the streets and trained her to be the queen's shadow. There had to be a reason."

Her chest tightened. A random girl off the streets. That's what she was, what she had always been. No amount of royal blood could change that. Just as Amanakar would always be the emperor's bastard.

"I found an old record of payments made to your grandmother. From the king. I deduced the rest."

Her mind whirled. He'd known all this time. Her greatest secret. "And you never told anyone?" she said, annoyed at how small her voice sounded.

He held her gaze. "I didn't."

"Why?" It didn't make any sense. He could have easily used that knowledge against her before now, against the queen.

"It's not... it's not something I would ever want to do to someone."

"It's not?" she said flatly.

"It's not," he repeated, his voice rumbling with emotion.

He knew. And he hadn't told. Hadn't used that information against her. And now he'd told her he knew. Revealed his greatest hand. She wanted to cry, to flee, to get as far away from here as she could, to escape the emotions raging inside her. Damn it, damn it, damn it. Why did he have this effect on her?

"And for the record," he said, "I don't think you're just a random girl off the streets."

Her heart gave a quick thud. She had to change the subject. They'd already strayed too far into forbidden territory. Territory that had never been a part of their game. Territory that was well beyond safe.

"Well, then," she said, doing her best to keep her voice steady. "Since you know my greatest secret, I'd say I'm owed yours."

"Oh, you are?" He crossed his arms, his eyes glinting with challenge. "If I'm any judge of our years working together—"

"Working together?" Her brows shot up. "*That's* what you call it?"

He grinned. It was the first real smile she'd ever seen from him. "I fully believe you know more about me than you're willing to admit."

Now it was her turn to smile. "It is my business to know these things, after all."

"And what is it that you know about me, Cass?"

She paused for a moment, studying him in the fading twilight. Tendrils of blue and amber filtered through the trees, casting shadows across his face. She remembered the way he had looked that night in Medira, dressed in black then too, an elegant fox mask over his eyes and nose. But here she could see his whole face, his eyes gleaming in the orange rays of the sun, the sharpness of his cheekbones, the line of dark stubble along his jaw. She could see the tiredness in his face, the flash of challenge and something else she couldn't bring herself to name when his gaze met hers.

"I know you're unhappy with your king."

Arphaxad's jaw tightened. "And what makes you say that?

"The Mediran king isn't exactly known for his . . . tact." She had to choose her words carefully. This thing that lay between them was too tenuous, too fragile. It could break apart at any moment. Arphaxad crossed his arms, waiting.

"You do a lot of cleaning up after him. I've seen several letters that have been . . . edited."

He snorted. "Of course you have."

She grinned, then leaned forward, surprised at the sudden earnestness in her voice. "I've also seen how you help people, Arphaxad. How you influence the king's directives toward the good of the people of Medira. From what I've seen, a lot of Medira's resources would end up in the palace rather than with the people who needed it if it weren't for you."

He shook his head. "And how do you know I'm not using my influence to benefit Medira? To benefit myself? Happy people don't tend to turn against their ruler." He paused. "Even if he is a bad one."

Now it was Cassandra's turn to snort. "If that's what you want me to think."

A muscle worked in his jaw. "No," he said, his voice filled with sudden intensity, "that's not what I want you to think."

"Good," she said.

He shook his head. "Working for someone you don't respect is . . ."

"It's admirable," she said firmly. "You have loyalty to more than just the king. You care about Medira, about its people, its future. That's more than I can say for most courtiers—most people—in both our kingdoms."

His mouth opened and closed. "Thank you," he said finally, and she could hear the sincerity in his voice, see it in his eyes.

Cassandra was the one to break his gaze. She turned and raised her bow again, sending another arrow toward the stump. This one missed entirely.

"Why didn't you shoot me that day in the palace?" His voice was low and earnest from beside her, devoid of the drawling sarcasm she was used to.

"It wouldn't have been any fun," she said as lightly as she could, reaching for another arrow. She couldn't look at him, couldn't let him see the truth on her face.

"Cass," he said. He laid a hand on her bow.

"It wouldn't have been," she insisted. "Plus, you saw me before I could get the shot off."

His hand was still on her bow. "We both know that's not true."

"Then why did you deposit me outside the palace after we'd both been taken out by the briar root?" She turned to face him now, her eyes blazing into his. This close, she could see the flecks of gold mixed in with the deep brown of his irises. He had a scar at his temple she'd never noticed before, the skin lighter than the rest. "You could have easily trussed me up and taken me to your king."

His eyes danced. "That wouldn't have been any fun."

"Ha," she said. "You have no answer either."

"I suppose not," he said softly. He took another step toward her. He was close now, so close that she could feel his breath on her face, see the darkness of his pupils, even in the fading light. "You never told your queen how I feel about my king," he said.

Her heart pounded maddeningly in her throat, but she didn't break his gaze, daring him to move closer, daring him to cross the wall that had been up between them for so long, too long. A boundary that out here, so far from the bounds of their kingdoms, suddenly seemed to be disintegrating.

"I did not." She could smell him now—a heady, earthy scent—and for a moment, she let herself wonder how it would feel to have his arms around her, to run her hands through his hair, to feel his warmth against her skin, his mouth on hers.

"Saving to use against me later?" he said softly. He tipped her chin up, his thumb skimming along her jaw.

She inhaled sharply. "Something like that," she breathed.

This was madness. This couldn't happen. But now, with his breath on her lips and the cool touch of his hands on her skin, she couldn't think at all.

A twig snapped in the bracken behind them, and they sprang apart. She whipped a couple of daggers from her belt as he did the same, then they stood back-to-back in the fading twilight of the forest as a group of men materialized from the trees. Inetians. Almost a dozen of them.

"Drop your weapons," one of the men called, his voice heavily accented. He was tall and brawny with golden-brown skin and a jagged scar across one cheek—the man Cassandra had seen talking to the white-haired chanter in the enclave.

A few more men materialized from the trees, their bows drawn. They were trapped.

Arphaxad tensed behind her. "On my signal," he breathed.

"Do it now!" the man said again.

Fire roared to life in her veins.

Arphaxad moved almost imperceptibly behind her. "Now."

In one swift motion, Cassandra sent a dagger into the leg of one of the men to her left. She heard a cry of pain as she whirled, sending the other toward another man deeper in the trees. Arphaxad must have done the same because she heard another shout as pandemonium broke loose. An arrow whizzed by her ear as she pulled another dagger from her belt. Her bow was too far away, and at this distance, it would be impossible to get a shot off.

"Hold your fire, you dolts!" the man who had commanded them to drop their weapons howled. "We need them alive!"

Cassandra rolled again as one of the men dove for her, then righted herself before kicking him in the groin. He doubled over as she skittered back, pulling a second dagger from her belt. Arphaxad wasn't the only one to be armed to the teeth.

She could see him a few yards away now, sparring with a man much larger than he was. The man swung for him, but Arphaxad ducked, moving as lithely as a cat. Cassandra rolled again, sending a dagger toward the man who was coming up behind Arphaxad. The man shrieked as the blade sliced through his shoulder. Arphaxad whirled and kicked the man in the stomach. The man doubled over.

"Thanks!" he called.

Cassandra didn't have any time to reply before a pair of arms wrapped around her waist, lifting her off the ground and crushing the air from her lungs. She gasped and stabbed her remaining dagger backward, deep into the leg of whoever was holding her. Her captor gave a yelp. His arms loosened slightly, just enough for Cassandra to slide downward, jamming her boot down on top of his foot.

The man yelped again, and she yanked at the dagger in his leg. He howled and collapsed to the ground, but the dagger slipped from her hands, slick with blood. She whirled, only to find another man coming after her with a long, jagged knife, much larger than her daggers. She tensed, waiting for him to get close enough to force him to drop the knife before it bit into her flesh.

The man gave a sudden howl and dropped to his knees, his knife scudding across the forest. Arphaxad was beside her then, his hands and the daggers clutched in them slick with blood. It spattered his face too in a spray of red. His eyes were wide, flaring with excitement, and he flashed her a huge, ridiculous grin.

"Come on." He panted, jerking his head toward the forest. "Let's get out of here."

She couldn't stop herself from sending an answering grin back. "Sounds good to me," she said.

He grunted. His jaw went slack, and Cassandra watched in horror as he slumped to the ground, clutching at his shoulder. An arrow protruded from his back. Cassandra catalogued its location, its damage, her heart pattering an intense rhythm in her chest. It was high, she realized in relief, too high to have hit anything major.

She swore, reaching for his good arm to drag him back to his feet. A knife-tip scraped against her neck, cold and hard. She froze, her chest heaving. She met Arphaxad's gaze—his eyes were dark with pain, and she could feel him shivering beneath her hand.

"I'll say it again," a gravelly voice said in her ear. "Drop. Your. Weapons."

Cassandra's stomach sank as she heard Arphaxad's daggers clatter to the ground. A moment later, hers did the same.

Chapter 6

Cassandra stumbled over an exposed root and landed on her face in the underbrush. She gasped as a stray branch stabbed into her ribcage. With her hands bound in front of her, she hadn't been able to catch herself at all.

"Get up!" one of the Inetians said roughly, helping her back to her feet. He was young, younger than she was, with deep bronze skin and a tall, muscular build. His black hair curled around his ears, and there was something in his demeanor that made him look incredibly boyish.

"Get up, yourself!" she snapped, then gasped as another one of the Inetians, this one skinny and angular, turned and yanked at her bound arms so that she stood face-to-face with him. Pain, hot and sharp, seared along her shoulders.

"Watch your mouth, girl," he snarled. Spittle splattered her cheek. "You're not in any position to be giving lip right now."

"Oh dear, I'm so terribly sorry," she drawled, leaning away from the stink of his breath. "Tell me how your humble servant should go about groveling."

The angular man shoved her backward, and she almost lost her footing again, but the younger man grabbed her arm to steady her.

"Watch her, Karim," the angular man snapped, before turning and stomping into the darkness ahead.

Cassandra seethed. She knew the smart thing to do was to shut up, to keep her head down, to find an opportunity to escape. But she was just too furious. Furious at this entire situation. Furious at the Inetians and their ridiculous plans. Furious that they'd shot Arphaxad. Furious that she had allowed him to distract her enough for all this to happen in the first place.

Heat flooded her body at the memory of his fingers skimming along her jaw, of his breath on her face, of the promise that had lingered in his gaze. Fury flared through her again. Damn it all. Her sister had been right. She *had* lost her head when it came to Arphaxad Ilin Serra.

The Inetians had made quick work of their weapons, removing most of her knives—they had missed one in her boot, but right now she had no way to reach it—and Arphaxad's as well. She had almost slugged the man beside her when one of the Inetians picked up her bow, pulled at the string, and then smugly slung it across his back. The *queen* had given her that.

When one of the men found the letters Cassandra had removed from the cave, she knew they were done for.

Arphaxad hadn't even cried out when his arms were tied in front of him, but Cassandra had seen the way his entire body jerked with pain. The Inetian who had first told them to drop their weapons—Paarsav, she'd learned—had ordered the arrow removed from Arphaxad's shoulder and the wound bound as the rest of the injured Inetians patched themselves up. No one had died.

"We don't want him dying on us," Paarsav had said. Arphaxad had given a coarse yell when the arrow was removed. Cassandra had followed his shout with a cascade of obscenities.

Now they moved in a quick line, heading back toward the ridge and the enclave in the valley below. It was dark now, too dark to see more than the dim outline of Arphaxad stumbling along ahead of her, his breath coming in ragged gasps with each step he took. Anger surged again, hot and sharp.

"Why don't you dimwits just open one of your magic doors to wherever you want to take us?" she snarled to the younger man, Karim, who walked closely behind her like a good guard dog. He had been one of the lucky few to escape injury. "Or are you too afraid after what happened to your friend earlier?"

His hand tightened around her arm, and he gave her a shake that made her teeth rattle. "Do you *want* to die?" he hissed under his breath. "If you keep on like that, they'll kill you, no questions asked."

"Don't let her get to you, Karim," Paarsav called from up ahead. "They'll be taken care of soon enough."

Taken care of. She ground her teeth together. She would not let them get to her either.

The blackness of the trees parted, revealing the soft orange glow of enchanted orb fire from the enclave below. Cassandra wanted to be anywhere but near that cave again, near the chanters and the wrongness of the rift.

They made their way slowly down the ridge and into the enclave. She could see silhouettes moving behind the oiled parchment in some of the huts. Doors opened quietly as the party limped through the enclave. People peered out for a moment before shutting their doors again tightly.

"So, why are you here, Karim?" she sneered. "You couldn't make it in Ineti? You had to resort to treachery to make a man of yourself?"

She could feel his hackles rising behind her. "Careful. You're treading on shaky ground," he said.

"Am I?" she said sweetly. "You don't have to tell me if it's truly too shameful."

Karim's hand closed around her arm. "Look," he said shortly, drawing her up beside him. "I have as many questions about this whole debacle as you. And as for why I'm here—my uncle was removed from his position in Talah for something he didn't do. And as a result, our entire family was cast out of the capital. The Inetian emperor is not a just man. He made it easy to turn against him. So don't go assuming things you know nothing about."

He released her and pushed her back along the trail in front of him. Cassandra stumbled again in the darkness, and for a moment, she felt sorry for him. He was young. He likely hadn't done anything to deserve that kind of treatment. But it didn't make what they were doing any more justifiable. "I'm sorry you felt you were forced into this," she said quietly.

Karim gave a gruff laugh, laced with surprise. "Thanks. But you have nothing to be sorry about."

Her heart ached. People always had reasons to justify their choices—that was something she had learned after years in this business—but it didn't make those choices right. She let her eyes wander to Arphaxad as he moved ahead of her, the angular man close on his heels. She could tell it took all his concentration to keep moving, to not let the pain overwhelm him. All over again, she wanted to rip every last one of them to shreds.

They stopped before the mouth of the cave, and Cassandra's stomach dropped. The entrance hadn't changed physically since she and Arphaxad had fled only a few hours before, but the sense of wrongness, of darkness, of power gone horribly wrong, had increased tenfold.

The angular Inetian shoved Arphaxad to his knees by the entrance. Arphaxad said something she couldn't catch, which earned him a cuff in the head.

"Hey!" Cassandra called out as Karim gestured for her to kneel beside Arphaxad. "You must feel like such a man when you hurt the injured and defenseless, huh? Does it make you feel powerful?"

"We should have killed you in the forest when we had the chance," the angular man spat.

"We don't know who they are yet and what they know," Karim said a bit uncertainly. "Paarsav seems to think they're higher ranking than they look. That bow is too nice to belong to a peasant. And they had information on them. Information that could give us away."

"Are you scared?" Cassandra taunted. They should never have been captured in the first place, not by these brutes, traitors to their emperor and country. How could she have been so stupid?

She glanced over at Arphaxad. He swayed beside her, his usually sharp gaze glazed and unfocused. Blood was seeping through the bandage around his shoulder. She swallowed, forcing back the fear that rose in her chest. He should never have been here, with her, in this stupid situation. If she hadn't let him get the best of her in Medira . . . But that wouldn't change anything about what the Inetians were doing.

"We'll get out of this," she said as much to herself as to him.

He turned his head and then winced. "I'm sorry, Cass," he whispered.

"Don't be," she snapped. "I got us into this mess. I'll get us out."

"Just you?" he said, a bit of the familiar sarcasm returning to his tone. "I think we've played equal roles in this."

"If that will make you feel better," she said, "then sure, it's all your fault." She thought she saw his mouth curve slightly.

"No talking!" the angular man commanded. Arphaxad ducked when the man's hand came toward his head. Cassandra almost launched herself at him at the same time that Karim said, "Quit it, Ankar." The man scowled but didn't try swinging again.

Paarsav had disappeared into the cave, and the others lingered outside, casting nervous glances toward the entrance. Most of them had probably seen what had happened inside earlier. She didn't blame them for wanting to get as far away from the place as possible. She had no desire to go in there again.

Paarsav emerged a few minutes later, the white-haired chanter—Gustav—following on his heels. Cassandra blinked. He was much younger than he had looked from afar, especially with that shock of white hair. He couldn't be more than ten years older than Cassandra.

"We found these stragglers up on the ridge," Paarsav was saying, jerking his head toward Cassandra and Arphaxad. "She had these on her." He showed the chanter the stack of papers Cassandra had removed from the cave.

Gustav's eyes snapped toward her—a piercing, icy blue, like the peoples of the Alliance in the south—and Cassandra only just kept herself from shuddering.

"They certainly know what we're doing here now," Paarsav continued.

The chanter moved toward them, his eyes narrowing as he approached. A heady sense of power clung to him, as well as the deep wrongness of the cave.

"Why did you come here?" His voice was gravelly, as if something had torn through his throat more than once over the years.

"We didn't mean to, sir." Cassandra simpered, widening her eyes and trying to drum up as much innocence in her voice as possible. "My fiancé and I got lost in the woods. We saw light coming from the valley and thought we must be near someplace that could help us!" She leaned toward Arphaxad, who gave her a skeptical sideways glance.

The chanter stared at her. "Just a girl and her fiancé, lost in the woods, armed to the teeth and able to wound six extremely well-trained soldiers."

"That's right," Cassandra replied.

"She's lying!" Paarsav snapped. The chanter cast him a tired glance.

"Where did you get this?" he asked, holding up the letters Cassandra had taken from the cave.

She shook her head. "I have no idea what those are," she said.

"Of course not," the chanter sighed. "Who do you work for?"

"She already told you," Arphaxad drawled, "we got lost in the woods and—"

The chanter waved his hand. "Please don't treat me like I know nothing. That's beyond me. And I had hoped it was beyond you." He leaned forward. "I'll say it again. Who do you work for?"

"That's none of your business," Cassandra said through gritted teeth.

The chanter turned to Paarsav and sighed. "Take them in. We're going to have to seal this place up anyway. Whether they're with Medira or Rendra or Ineti doesn't really matter, as long as they're not alive to get their information out."

Fear stabbed through her chest. Seal the place up? What did *that* mean?

Paarsav jerked his head toward the cave entrance, and Karim pulled on Cassandra's arm, helping her to her feet.

"How do you know we haven't gotten the information out already?" Cassandra blurted. "We know who you are, what you're trying to do. And it's a coward's road."

The chanter turned to face her. His lips curved. "So now you change your tune," he said. "Not so lost, I think."

"Not lost at all," she snapped, shaking Karim's hand off her arm. He let her go but didn't move away. "What's your ploy?" She straightened her shoulders, meeting his icy gaze with more confidence than she felt. "What could Amanakar have promised to make you think overturning the Inetian emperor was remotely a good idea? That teaching these . . . these boneheads magic that they will clearly misuse and destroy the rest of us wasn't ridiculous?"

The chanter's lips twisted. "You think you understand us, what we want, what we're striving for. But you do not," he said coldly.

"We might if you told us," Cassandra said. "Medira, Rendra, even Ineti, might help if you asked for it."

The chanter shook his head, his eyes incredibly cold. "You would like to think that, wouldn't you?" he said. "That, in my experience, is not the way the world works."

Fury surged through her again in a frightening wave. She understood why the chanters might feel jaded, scorned, oppressed by the world—they believed so strongly in something, and they had been cast out again and again because of it. But it still didn't explain why they'd strike a bargain like this.

"Then tell me," Cassandra pleaded. "You don't have to do this."

Paarsav shuffled uncomfortably behind the chanter, exchanging looks with the other Inetians. They smiled in a way Cassandra didn't like. "That's all I needed to know."

He nodded to Paarsav. "Bring them in. We can't hold it for much longer."

Paarsav nodded to Karim and the angular man. Karim closed his fingers around her arm again, but he hesitated, as if torn by what they were about to do.

"Get off her!" Arphaxad cried, lunging to his feet. The angular man tapped him lightly on his injured shoulder, and Arphaxad doubled over, letting out an involuntary roar of pain.

"Stop it!" Cassandra snarled, trying and failing to pull herself from Karim's grasp. Karim just dragged her blankly toward the cave entrance, even as she thrashed and screamed. She didn't care that she wasn't dignified. Getting away was all that mattered now.

The pale chanter led the way, followed by Paarsav, then Cassandra and Karim, and Arphaxad and the angular man. The inside of the cave was more oppressive than she remembered—the darkness, the wrongness, pressing in on them as they were dragged along toward the cavern with its door and the rift and its horror.

This wasn't how this was supposed to go. She had to get back to Rendra, to the queen. She couldn't leave her sister alone in the world again. This was not how she was going to die!

The ground shuddered for a moment, and they all paused to brace themselves. Karim swore. Fear sliced through her chest. The sound of the chanters rose from the cavern ahead, a cacophony of voices, the cadence jarring, shattering, as if they were slowly breaking apart, losing their battle with whatever had been torn apart in the explosion earlier that day.

"Something's wrong," Karim muttered uneasily.

"You think?" Paarsav snapped as the ground shuddered again. The chanter said nothing.

She could hear Arphaxad's labored breathing behind her, and she wanted to reach out and touch him, to let him know that she was here, that she would get them out.

The cavern opened up just as it had before. Below, Cassandra could see the twelve doors winking at intervals around the space. And there, toward the back, was the ring of chanters, their hands clasped, swaying as they spoke their parts, the words and cadence weaving together in the air, crackling with power, before it was funneled toward the thing that hung at the back of the cavern—that black, roaring nothingness.

"Move!" Paarsav barked, following the pale chanter as he made his way carefully down the wooden staircase set into the stone.

Karim looked like he was going to throw up. For a moment, Cassandra thought she might have a chance to break free, to flee, to slip into the darkness of the cave, dart through one of the doors and disappear. But there was Arphaxad bleeding behind her, and she knew she could never do it, could never leave him here to die.

The pulsating nausea from before returned as they neared the ring of chanters. Cassandra could see the sweat standing out on their foreheads, the exhaustion in their faces—the terror as well.

Karim forced her onto her knees as close to the rift as he dared go. She hardly noticed the stone biting into her knees; the rift was there, close, a yawning, horrible thing. She wanted to run, to scream, to get as far away from here as possible. Arphaxad was forced down beside her.

He looked even worse now, his face pale, his gaze wandering. Rage flared in her again. She would not let him die.

The pale chanter shouted something Cassandra couldn't understand to the swaying ring. For a moment, the chanting faltered, then came back in a frenzied roar. The ground shook again, this time more violently, and Cassandra couldn't help the cry that escaped her throat.

"Get out!" Paarsav roared. The angular man didn't have to be told twice.

Karim lingered, looking down at her, his gaze conflicted. Cassandra tipped her chin at him, her eyes flaring defiantly. In a movement so quick Cassandra almost missed it, Karim slipped a knife from his belt. Then he was beside her, hastily sawing through the bonds around her wrists. Blood rushed painfully through her hands as the ropes fell away, and he knelt next to Arphaxad to do the same.

"What are you doing, soldier? I said, get out of here!" Paarsav roared again.

"Thank you, Karim," Cassandra said, a lump forming in her throat as the ropes around Arphaxad's wrists fell away too. Karim gave them a grim nod.

"Here," he said, shoving the knife he'd used to cut their ropes into her hand. "You need this more than I do. I hope it offers you some sort of protection." Then he turned and bolted after Paarsav.

Cassandra's fingers closed around her knife. As she slipped it into her boot, she suddenly felt as if there might be some hope in this darkness after all.

"We have to get out of here!" Arphaxad yelled beside her, scrabbling to his feet. The earth shook again, and a scattering of stones rained down from above. Cassandra gripped his arm to steady herself. Blood was flowing through her stiff hands now, and she had to grit her teeth to keep from crying out from the pain.

A hand came down on her shoulder, shoving her back down. Cassandra raised her head, locking gazes with the pale chanter. He shook his head slowly, as if daring her to get to her feet. "Stay down," he growled. "You're not going anywhere."

Some of the chanters broke the circle and fled for the stairs toward the cave entrance. The circle tightened as the chanters left behind joined hands.

"We have to bring the roof down now!" someone shouted. The chanting rose into a frenzied crescendo as more chanters peeled off and made a dash for the entrance.

Cassandra gave a cry of rage and desperation as the ground shook again, more violently than it had before, and she was tossed to the ground.

"Cass!" she heard Arphaxad cry. His hand closed around her arm, and he dragged her backward, toward the rift.

"What are you doing?" she cried, but her voice was swallowed up by the deep rumble of the roof coming down around them.

And then he was throwing his body over hers, her head cradled between his hands. His face, his body, was so close, she could feel the beating of his heart.

"Get off me!" she cried, pummeling her fists against his chest. "You can't do this, Phax!"

"Keep your head down, damn it!" he snapped as debris rained down around them. The cave was collapsing. And with it, their final hope of escape. She gave a deep cry of frustration. This was not how it would end. Not after what they'd seen. Not after what they had found out. No one was safe—not with Amanakar's idiotic plan. Not with the white-haired chanter egging him on.

A sob burst from her chest as Arphaxad grunted and the ground roared beneath them. He couldn't do this, protect her like this. She couldn't let him.

"Stay still," he murmured in her ear. "I've got you, Cass."

Damn him. She clutched at the dark material of his tunic, pulling him closer. If this was the way she had to die, it wasn't the worst way to go, locked together with him. As they had always been. As she had always wanted it to be.

The roaring grew to a deafening crescendo as debris rained down around them. The earth shook, and Cassandra buried her face in Arphaxad's good shoulder to keep herself from screaming. She wanted to memorize the feel of him, the heat of him, the way his hands were stroking her hair, the way her body molded perfectly to his. She felt him shudder as debris bounced off his back, and as he pulled her closer, she thought she heard him murmur her name.

Then, in a great, shuddering roar, the world turned black.

Chapter 7

She wasn't dead.

A shrill, incessant ringing stung her ears, and dust coated her eyes and her mouth and every crevice of her body. But she wasn't dead.

It had taken an age for the ground to stop moving, for the thunderous sound of the mountain crumbling above them to cease, for the dust to settle and for the world to right. She'd kept her face pressed into Arphaxad's shoulder, breathing in the scent of him, waiting for the end, waiting for the moment they would be buried beneath the earth. No one would ever know what had happened to them. Her sister—she bit back the sob that threatened to burst from her chest.

But the end had never come, just a cascade of dust that had coated her hair and her arms and her clothes, every place that Arphaxad wasn't covering with his own body. She'd pulled her face back from his shoulder. A wall of earth and stone rose hardly half a foot from them, stretching overhead like a dome.

"Phax," she rasped. Her throat was dry, and it came out sounding like little more than a croak.

He stirred and lifted his head from her shoulder. His dark hair had turned a dusty gray just as she knew hers had, and she could see a thin red line where a stray stone had bitten into his cheek. "Cassandra?" The way he said her name, with such a tinge of hopeful joy, sent a shock wave through her body.

"I'm here," she said.

"Are you all right?" he breathed, running a hand along her hair, as if to make sure for himself.

She coughed again and then nodded, shivering beneath his touch. He was still so close, his body pressed against hers, his fingers threading lightly through her hair.

He coughed this time, his entire body shuddering with the pain. She suddenly remembered his shoulder, the arrow, the blood. She swore and pushed him off her. The wound was still bleeding—she could tell by the blood darkening the bandage the Inetians had hastily applied.

"You—why did you do that?" she asked, staring at him in the strange, ambient light. He'd shielded her when the world was crumbling around them. He'd been ready to trade his life for hers.

"I couldn't stand it if you'd died," he said softly.

His words hit her like the ton of earth that hovered above their heads. For a moment, she stared at him. He couldn't just *say* that to her. Not here, not like this. Not when they were both covered in dirt and sweat and blood, and a rift of horrors pulsed at their backs. "Your life is not worth more than mine!" she snapped. Then she blinked. Light. They could see.

Her head jerked toward the rift. It was only a few feet from them, a terrible black thing, but its edges gave off a strange, otherworldly glow. Arphaxad followed her gaze.

"It worked," he said incredulously, staring at the darkness of the rift. "I thought it might."

She remembered with startling clarity the way he'd dragged them closer to the rift rather than away as the roof had started to come down around them. He'd been working off a hunch, but it had been right. The rift, whatever power was emanating from it, had created this little pocket of space beneath the massive weight of the earth.

"Well, that's . . . something," she said. The blackness pulsed as she stared at it, a swirling mass of nothingness, of wrongness, enough to drive one mad. She tore her gaze away, the nausea rising again in her stomach.

"So, what now?" she asked. She met his gaze across the small space, and in that moment, the reality of their situation hit. The rift might be holding back the weight of the entire mountain, but it hadn't changed anything about their predicament. If anything, it had made it worse. They had no food, no water, and what little air was left down here would likely run out in a few hours.

They were going to die here after all.

Arphaxad seemed to realize it at the same time she did, and he slumped down to the uneven stone floor. He winced and cradled his bad arm.

"I'm sorry," he murmured, running a hand through his soot-covered hair. "I never thought—"

"Never thought what?" Cassandra asked. Tension buzzed in her fingertips. They couldn't just sit here. They had to do something to find a way out. Anything.

"I never thought it would end this way."

She stared at him for a moment. "It's *not* going to end this way," she said vehemently. Rendra had to know what Amanakar was planning. Medira had to be warned, and so did Ineti. They couldn't allow these scums of the earth to *win*.

"Oh really?" he said, gesturing around them pointedly. "You think there's a way out of here?"

"We'll figure it out," she snapped.

"Come on, Cass," he said. He sounded drained, beaten.

"No!" she rounded on him, indignation rising in her gut. "I have never once seen you give up before, Arphaxad. What's gotten into you?"

He let out a bleak "ha". "They left us to die in here, Cassandra. In fact, I'm sure they already think we're dead. They dropped an entire forsaken mountain on us!"

Cassandra ground her teeth together. "I've beaten better odds before on my own," she said. "But now I have you. That must count for something."

His head snapped up, and he stared at her for a long moment, his gaze unreadable. Then he gave her a soft smile. "You have no idea how much I want it to count."

Her heart gave a fierce thud, and the space between them seemed to grow smaller, until he felt too close, too intense, and she wanted to scream and cry and rage. But most of all, with the way he was looking at her now, she wanted to live.

"I will not let them win," she said at last.

"I believe you," he said.

She let out a cry of frustration and kicked her boot against the wall. She swore as her boot clinked against something unforgiving, something harder than the stone surrounding them, sending a shockwave of pain up her leg. Stupid, stupid, stupid.

She paused and dropped to her knees, using her aching fingers to swipe at the dirt where her foot had made contact. Her heart stuttered as she revealed the first sign of hope. A small slice of black glimmered from beneath the gray soot. It was metal. Forged metal. A tiny part of a man-made frame—one of the twelve doors that had glimmered around the cavern. A door that could lead them out of here.

"It's here!" she cried, pulling more frantically at the stones. She could see the corner of the frame pushing from the debris. Her fingers throbbed as she pulled out another rock, and the shimmering outline of the door became visible.

"What?" Arphaxad said. He pulled himself shakily to his feet.

"One of the enclave's doors," she said breathlessly as she hauled another stone away, praying the space wouldn't collapse around them. "We could use it to get out."

Arphaxad was beside her in an instant, helping her heave stones aside as quickly as he could with his damaged shoulder.

Sweat pooled down her neck, slipping beneath her grimy tunic and down her back. They had to clear enough to be able to slip through. Right now, they could see enough to push an arm through. The door *had* to work, *had* to accept them. It *had* to lead them out of here, away, and not tumbling out into some nameless void. It was the only chance they were likely to have.

One of the stones they tossed back shuddered, then skittered backward of its own accord and went spiraling into the rift with a sick popping sound. Arphaxad swore, and Cassandra grabbed his good arm as the bubble around them shuddered and the ground began to shift.

Cassandra's ears popped as a wave of power poured out of the rift, forcing the weight of the mountain back. A cry of frustration tore from her chest, then changed into one of elation as the stones and rocks and earth moved outward. The entire weight of the mountain was *moving*.

But the power surging from the rift didn't weaken. If anything, it got stronger. The earth shook, tossing them both back to the floor. With a ghastly crunch, the forged-metal frame bent, its sides compacting under the pressure. The shimmer within the frame flickered out for one dreadful moment, and then came reluctantly back, holding steady for one second, then two.

"We have to go now!" Arphaxad shouted as the earth shuddered again. Cassandra let out a string of expletives as he grabbed her arm, and shouting, dragged them through the door.

They tumbled out into cold, night air. Cassandra stumbled a few feet and almost lost her footing when her boot caught against something hard. Arphaxad's fingers tightened around her arm, pulling her up and back against his chest. They stood there for a moment, staring at each other with wide eyes, breathing heavily.

A cool breeze picked up in the branches above them, and Cassandra almost laughed in delight. She'd never take something so mundane for granted again. The door had spat them out beneath a rocky outcrop, dark forest spreading out on either side, familiar pines jutting wildly into the air. Somewhere in the distance, a stream babbled its way through the night.

"We did it," Arphaxad said giddily, giving her a stupid grin.

"And you thought we were dead," she said, her own grin just as ridiculous.

The door shimmered behind them in the moonlight. It flickered again like it had back in the cave, and Cassandra caught a whiff of sulfur as tendrils of black strayed across its face. There was a strange crackling noise, and then the door winked out entirely, leaving nothing behind but the empty metal frame.

They both stared at it for a moment, and a mix of relief and horror rolled through Cassandra like a tidal wave.

A strange, wholly inappropriate laugh bubbled up from somewhere in her belly, and she had to force it back. They were alive. They were *alive*. Any later and they wouldn't have made it out at all.

Arphaxad's face was as streaked with soot as hers was, but even with his usually dark hair ashen and his olive skin pale with dust, he was just about the most wonderful thing she had ever seen.

"Where do you think we are?" she asked. The moon was full, and even in this darkness, she was able to make out the ragged old-growth pines stretching out around them.

"The enclave must have made it here for a reason," Arphaxad said.

Cassandra nodded. "The trees look the same as they did on the ridge above the valley. We can't be too far from the enclave."

Arphaxad stared down the slope for a moment, his lips pursed.

"There's a river or steam of some sort below," Cassandra continued, watching him. She knew enough about the Malathi pass, but this was Arphaxad's territory.

His head snapped up. "I think I know where we are," he said, and struck out down the slope toward the sound of the moving water.

Cassandra followed him, careful not to lose her footing in the darkness and send them both tumbling down the slope. She was the queen's shadow, but she wasn't invincible as she had so recently learned.

The high summer chorus of cicadas rose through the forest, interrupted intermittently by the quick chirp of a toad or the soft bray of a deer somewhere in the trees. Cassandra knew that cougars moved through these parts of the woods as well, and she kept her hand on the knife Karim had slid to her before he left the cave. She'd never expected that sort of kindness from one of the betraying Inetians. Perhaps it had been pity. She wondered if he'd made it out in the end.

They reached the bottom of the slope where a shallow river glittered in the moonlight. A thick hedge of ferns lined the banks on either side, and she could see the dark, glistening mounds of rocks dotted through the moving water. Suddenly, Cassandra realized how thirsty she was. Without a second thought, she followed Arphaxad to the edge and dipped her fingers into the icy water. She splashed water on her face, trying to get as much of the grime off as she could before scooping the water into her mouth. It was cold, tasting faintly of snowmelt from higher in the mountains.

She sat back on her heels for a moment, watching Arphaxad as he drank like a dying man. She grimaced. Perhaps he was. They had to get him medical attention for his shoulder. He was still losing blood, though the flow seemed slower now.

Arphaxad looked up at her, his eyes shining. "This has to be the Malathi river," he said. "If we follow it down, we should end up at a Mediran military outpost."

Her heart gave a thud. A Mediran military outpost. One of the last places she wanted to be. "Great," she said, mustering as much cheer as she could. "We need to get your shoulder looked at."

They made their way along the riverbank, keeping their eyes peeled for any movement in the trees. With the doors in the cave destroyed, she didn't think the chanters would be moving in these parts, especially at this time of night. But she couldn't know for sure. And after what they'd just been through, they couldn't take any more chances.

Exhaustion ground deep into her bones as they rounded another bend in the river. Arphaxad stopped, and she slowed her pace behind him. Finally, through the trees, there was a haze of orange enchanted orb fire and the outline of a tall wooden fence. The outpost.

Arphaxad gave a whoop of triumph. "We made it!"

Cassandra said nothing. He had every right to rejoice. They had survived the impossible. But she wasn't certain a Mediran outpost in the mountains could ever be considered safe for the Rendran queen's shadow.

But right now, she didn't particularly care, as long as they dressed Arphaxad's wound and let her sleep for a year. Maybe two.

The outpost wasn't large, not in this remote of an area, but Cassandra could see sentries with bows posted along the walls, peering into the forest. She and Arphaxad darted onto the wagon-rutted road as they neared the outpost, and Arphaxad raised his good arm as they stepped slowly toward the shuttered gates.

"Who goes there?" one of the sentries called from his post on top of the wall.

"I'm Arphaxad Ilin Serra," Arphaxad said. He reached beneath his shirt and pulled something out—it glinted gold in the moonlight. "I bear the seal of the king."

Cassandra's lips curved. Another thing the inept Inetians had missed when they'd searched them.

There was silence for a moment, followed by the scrape of a metal bolt being drawn back, then the gate creaked open enough to let a person pass through.

"Arphaxad?" A tall, broad-shouldered man with a thick beard stepped out from behind the gate. "It's been an absolute age. I didn't expect to see you in these parts for—" His eyes widened as he took in the blood darkening the bandage around Arphaxad's shoulder. "By the Archer, man, you need a doctor!"

"I think you're probably right," Arphaxad said. He took a stumbling step forward and collapsed.

Chapter 8

Cassandra darted forward as Arphaxad slumped to the dirt. The man at the gate was beside them in an instant, reaching for Arphaxad's wounded shoulder.

"Careful," Cassandra said. "He's had an arrow in the back."

"Right," the man said, and shifted to help Cassandra pull Arphaxad to his feet. Arphaxad's head lolled forward, and he let out a moan as Cassandra angled herself beneath his good arm, letting his weight settle on her shoulder.

"Stretcher! We've got wounded!" the broad man shouted toward the sentries at the top of the wall. His declaration was met with shouts of affirmation, and he and Cassandra dragged Arphaxad through the gate and into the outpost. A moment later, two soldiers in the red and green of Medira met them with a wooden stretcher.

"I can walk," Arphaxad protested weakly, but he didn't fight when Cassandra pushed him gently down. His head dropped back, and his eyes fluttered closed. Cassandra's heart gave a sickening thud, and she slid her fingers down his arm to squeeze his hand. He opened his eyes for a moment and gave her a quick smile as if to say, "I'll be all right."

Cassandra kept close to the stretcher as the two soldiers lifted it and set out across the muddy cobblestone courtyard toward a squat building at the back of the outpost. Inside was a dim room lit by a pair of orbs of enchanted fire set on a workbench in the back. A long table rested in the middle of the room, and beside it was a sagging shelf holding glass vials of various herbs and colorful liquids. A soldier with graying hair jumped to his feet when they entered, and immediately directed the soldiers to set Arphaxad on the table. They did so with a clatter, and Cassandra almost barked something unpleasant at them.

"Gently!" the gray-haired man said with an exasperated wave of his hand. "What happened to him?" he asked, pivoting to face Cassandra.

"An arrow, a few hours ago now. I don't think the bleeding ever stopped."

The man—who could only be the outpost healer—grimaced and leaned over to get a better look at the bloody bandage around Arphaxad's shoulder.

"Brace yourself, son," he said grimly. "This is going to hurt." It was only when he started cutting away the blood-soaked bandage that Cassandra's stomach heaved, and she fled the room.

She burst into the cool night air and pressed her back against the rough side of the building, tipping her head back so it rested against the calloused wood. Stars spread above her in a swath of unending brilliance, the constellation of the Archer twinkling in the northeast. She squeezed her eyes shut, fighting against the panic that threatened to overwhelm her. What was her sister doing now back in Rendra? Was she wondering what had happened to her?

She swallowed hard against the lump in her throat. She'd lost her bow, the one thing that meant something to her. She'd lost the correspondence she'd taken from the cave, their only proof of what Amanakar was planning. And now she was cornered in a Mediran military outpost, surrounded by people who thought she was the enemy, no matter what kind of strange truce had existed between her and Arphaxad today. She slammed her fist against the wall behind her, wincing as her skin scraped against the wood.

It was stupid to stay here, she realized. Stupid to remain in a position where she could easily be caught and taken to the Mediran palace. She didn't think Arphaxad would stoop that low, not after what they'd been through, but she couldn't say the same for the other soldiers.

But she couldn't just leave either, not until she knew he was all right. Not when she was this exhausted. And not until she was sure their information would make it into the right hands.

Her mind fluttered to that midsummer night not long ago at the Mediran palace when she had looked up at a similar sky. She'd been with Arphaxad then too, dancing with him beneath the moonlight, her fingers in his, his hand pressing against her back, his breath on her skin. She fought back the sob that welled up in her throat. She had almost died today. More than once. And now he might be dying too.

She hauled in a deep breath and let it out slowly, then did it again, and again, just as Andre had taught her.

The door to the infirmary opened to her left, and the man who had met them at the gate stepped out. For the first time, Cassandra noticed that he wore the green stripe of a Mediran commander on the right shoulder of his uniform. He paused when he saw her, and she straightened.

"I'm sorry," he said after a moment. "I don't believe we've had the pleasure."

"Cassandra," she said after a moment. She wasn't sure what Arphaxad had managed to tell him, if anything, but she couldn't risk contradicting his story.

He nodded. "Ramon Castez. I'm the commander of this outpost and a long-time friend of Ilin Serra's."

Cassandra took his offered hand and shook it. His palm was rough, but his grip was firm. "Thank you for your help," she said.

Castez gave a short nod. He was wary of her, she realized. And he had every right to be. "How are you ... connected ... to him?"

"We work together," she said vaguely. She didn't even have to lie about that—at least for the moment.

He glanced toward the infirmary door and then back, his eyes sharp, as if he didn't know what to make of her. He looked like he very much preferred a more concrete answer than that. He opened his mouth, then shut it again. "What happened?" he asked instead.

Cassandra hesitated. Castez said he was a long-time friend, but until she heard it from Arphaxad himself, she had to tread carefully. "It's ... a long story," she said finally.

Castez pressed his lips together, but, to her relief, didn't probe further. "I'll find a place where you can wash up and rest for the night." He followed Cassandra's gaze toward the infirmary door. "He'll be a while. The wound needs to be cleaned and dressed. Encar is as good as it gets, but it won't be pretty."

Exhaustion ground deep into her bones as she followed Castez to the other end of the outpost and into another squat wooden building. He opened a door on the right, and Cassandra stepped inside. The room was sparse. A narrow bed with a brown, threadbare blanket sat on one end, and a low cabinet and ancient writing desk were pushed against the window on the other.

"One of the officers' rooms," Castez said. "He's been back in the capital for a few weeks. It's yours for as long as you need it."

"Thank you," Cassandra said. Castez gave her a nod, then stepped back into the hallway and closed the door behind him.

Cassandra was quick to push the deadbolt in place, then pressed her ear to the crack between the door and the wall. As she'd expected, Castez had posted a guard at the door. A muscle jerked in her jaw, and she dragged the cabinet in front of the door, barricading it from the inside. She couldn't risk anyone trying anything, not when she was alone in an enemy camp and tipping into a realm beyond exhaustion.

There was a washbasin in one corner, and she did her best to get as much of the grime off her body as she could. The water was almost black when she was done. She pulled her hair out of its careful knot and ran her fingers through it in an attempt to get the worst of the snarls out. After a few minutes, she gave up, then finally, *finally*, collapsed onto the bed, and despite the lumpy mattress and the camp full of enemy soldiers and the fact that she'd almost died more than once and that Arphaxad might just be dying now and that she really, *really* didn't want to think about why that made her feel so hollow inside, she fell into a deep, dreamless sleep.

***

She awoke to a knock on her door. She blinked the sleep out of her eyes, and for a moment, couldn't remember where she was. Sunlight streamed in through the window, illuminating the threadbare blanket, the dull wooden boards of the walls, and the cabinet barricading the door.

She shot up as everything came back in a rush—Amanakar, the chanters, Arphaxad. A heaviness descended on her chest, and she swung her legs over the side of the bed. At least she'd been left to sleep.

"Who is it?" she called, reaching for her boots, which she had kicked off the night before. Her dagger was still there—the one the Inetians hadn't found—and Karim's dagger with its black handle stamped with the Inetian sigil of a golden bird was still in her boot.

"Cass," a familiar voice said softly. "It's me."

Relief swept through her like a tidal wave, and she did her best to school her face into a neutral expression before she dragged back the cabinet with a horrible scraping sound, pulled the deadbolt, and opened the door.

Arphaxad stood on the other side, his left arm secured in a sling. The guard was nowhere to be seen. He wore a fresh uniform in the red and green colors of Medira. There were dark circles under his eyes, and the stubble along his jaw had progressed into a full shadow. His mouth was tipped in that familiar, arrogant smile, which made her heart give a traitorous thump.

"Did you sleep well last night?" he drawled, his gaze flicking to the cabinet she hadn't pushed all the way back in place.

She glared at him. "I did, thank you very much. No thanks to you, leaving me alone in a Mediran outpost."

He arched a brow at her. "You alone in a Mediran military installation is exactly what I was worried about."

She smirked. It wasn't everyday she was granted free access to a Mediran military installation, even if it were one as remote as this. "Too bad your friend oh so helpfully posted a guard at my door."

Arphaxad blinked. So, he didn't know. "Smart man," he said finally.

"And to think, I was so worried about you."

"You were worried about me?" His smile broadened. "Cass, I'm flattered."

"Well, I'm not anymore." She crossed her arms, warmth rising to her cheeks. Her eyes traveled to his sling. "No longer at death's door, I take it?"

He shrugged, then winced as if he had forgotten about his shoulder. "No, thank the Archer. Encar is good at what he does. He had a healing tincture he'd traded for with an Alliance caravan. Seems to be working, at least for the pain."

"Better than nothing," she said.

They were quiet for a moment, each waiting for the other to say something.

"We'll need to give a report to Ramon," Arphaxad said finally, his eyes skittering away from her. "He's in charge of the outpost here and of dealings with the enclave. Our first line of defense."

Cassandra nodded. They had to tell someone. Figure out what kind of force they could gather to stop the idiocy of the Inetians. They'd already wasted enough time.

And then Arphaxad would go back to the Mediran palace, and Cassandra would go back to her queen. That was all that was left.

Arphaxad shifted uncomfortably. "We'll need to get the information to the king. Do something about the Inetian ambassador. It's going to be . . . tricky."

That was an understatement. "Rendra will need to know, too," she said.

"Of course," he said quickly. "I would hope this leads to some sort of . . . of alliance."

She stared at him. An alliance between Rendra and Medira. It had been unthinkable for so long. Something more than a tenuous peace would be . . . incredible. Her mind started to turn, as if it were just waking up. Why hadn't she thought of that? Maybe, just maybe, they finally had the pieces to stitch the broken bonds between the two countries together. A greater cause to unite them. A tiny flame of hope lit in Cassandra's chest.

"I'll do my best to encourage the king to send an envoy to Rendra as soon as possible," Arphaxad said.

"Medira would stoop so low?" she teased.

His mouth tipped. "You can be insufferable, you know."

"I don't think I'm alone in that," she said.

A group of soldiers clomped down the hall from the direction of the barracks, slapping and cajoling each other as they went. Cassandra tensed as they passed. A few of the men blinked when they saw her, clearly not expecting a woman in their midst.

Arphaxad glanced over his shoulder as the men piled out the door and into the cobblestone courtyard. When they were gone, he turned back to her, meeting her gaze with a sudden intensity. "You have my protection here, Cass," he said. "I hope you know that."

A shiver moved through her at the intensity in his voice. She believed him. Of course she did. But she wasn't so sure the rest of the Mediran army would feel the same.

"Come on," she said, pushing past him. "We should probably find Castez. And some food. I'm starving."

***

An hour later, Castez leaned back in his chair and let out a long, slow breath. "How in the name of the Archer did we miss that?" he asked.

He was perched behind a heavy mahogany desk in a room twice the size of the one Cassandra had slept in. A shelf of leather-bound books leaned on the wall behind him, and a swath of gold-embroidered curtains adorned the window. A red velvet chaise sat under it, and Cassandra caught a hint of cigar smoke clinging to the fabric.

Arphaxad shook his head. "The chanters are going to great lengths to hide what's going on. If I hadn't received a"—he cast a quick glance at Cassandra—"a tip from one of my sources, we would still have no idea."

Cassandra almost snorted. A tip from one of his sources indeed.

Castez rifled through a stack of paper inscribed with neat letters in thick black ink. "We'll need to gather a significant force to raid the enclave. They may think you're dead, but my guess is the accident put them on high alert."

"We've seen what havoc they can wreak when they don't know they're being watched," Arphaxad said. "I don't want to know what kind of horror they can stir up when they do."

Cassandra listened to the two men draft plans for how to best draw out the rogue Inetians without tipping off the chanters. She didn't feel like she had the right to interject, though Arphaxad kept glancing at her for confirmation every now and then. This was his territory. And the last thing she wanted to give away to Castez was who she really worked for. Castez seemed to take her presence for granted now, which showed just how much he trusted Arphaxad.

She also wasn't sure why Arphaxad hadn't kicked her out yet. Even with the possibility of a Rendran–Mediran alliance on the table, there wasn't much more she could do here. He'd quipped earlier about the dangers of leaving her to roam a Mediran military outpost on her own, but he surely couldn't expect to watch her at every moment. She wasn't complaining. She wasn't ready to leave yet. And she didn't want to think too hard about exactly why that was.

Arphaxad sat back in the chair beside her and ran his good hand through his hair. His face was ashen. Cassandra wanted to kick him back to the infirmary and make him rest. He'd taken an arrow to the back not even twenty-four hours ago.

"Inetian traitors in our midst," Castez said with a shake of his head. "I bet you're glad to have sniffed this out before your wedding, eh, Arphaxad?"

Cassandra's stomach dropped. Wedding?

Arphaxad went rigid beside her as Castez rose to grab a glass decanter of amber liquid from the shelf behind his desk. He poured a splash into a glass and then turned to hand it to Arphaxad, who accepted it woodenly.

Castez shook his head. "Who'd have thought the likes of you would end up marrying an Inetian princess?"

Cassandra's body went cold. A strange roaring built in her ears, and she could see Castez's mouth moving, but no sound was coming out. It was as if she were underwater, sinking slowly downward into a bottomless pool.

Marry the Inetian princess.

Arphaxad was marrying the Inetian princess.

Her fingers pressed numbly against the fabric of her tunic. How could she have been so stupid? All this time she had just *assumed* it was the Mediran king who was marrying the princess. But of course, it wasn't. It could never have been. The king had never shown much interest in marriage, and he was far too old to be thinking of marriage now. He didn't have an heir, but his next oldest brother was well-positioned to take over if anything happened to him, and the king seemed all too happy to let him.

And Arphaxad. He was the perfect candidate. He was well-connected, handsome, charming, and far enough from the throne that it was unlikely he would ever ascend to it. The perfect man for the job. How had she not seen it?

Her gaze shifted from where it had been fixed on a knot in one of the floorboards, and she found herself staring directly into his eyes. It was suddenly hard to breathe.

How could she have been so blind? The truth was so candescently obvious.

And then, in a blazing flash of clarity, she understood. She hadn't *wanted* to know because then she'd have been forced to face the terrifying truth that she'd tried so hard to ignore: that she was in love with Arphaxad Ilin Serra. And she had been for a long, long time.

Her mind whirled. Her body thundered with the knowledge, and for a moment, the world was right and whole and good.

She was in love with Arphaxad Ilin Serra.

She remembered the way he had pulled her close as they danced in the Mediran palace, how much she had wanted that night never to end, and all the times before that when they'd clashed, and he'd made her feel more furious and more alive than she'd ever felt before. How his fingers had traced her jaw in the forest outside the enclave, and how much she'd wished he would just kiss her already and that they could pretend the complicated world around them didn't exist, even for a few exhilarating moments.

But she had never allowed herself to dwell on it, to comprehend it, because it was too impossible. Too dangerous. He was not someone she could afford to fall in love with.

But it was already too late.

He would be marrying the Inetian princess in a few weeks' time, cementing Medira's relationship with Ineti. Forging an important alliance. And she would go home to Rendra. And what? Forget him? That would be impossible considering they were the only two people who knew about Amanakar and the enclave. And if this were truly the thing that would bring Rendra and Medira together, then . . .

"Yep," was all Arphaxad said. He tried to catch her gaze, and there was something in it, a question, something she didn't want to see, didn't want to know. She jerked her gaze away from him. She couldn't look at him—not now, not when she was sure her feelings were etched plainly on her face.

"I hear she's quite a beauty too, you lucky man." Castez grinned.

Cassandra stood up and walked out of the room.

Footsteps sounded behind her as she stepped out into the harsh midday sun. The sun was well above the horizon now, trudging toward noon. Soldiers lingered in the courtyard, a few sparring in one corner with short swords, their uniforms dark with sweat, but none of them spared her much attention.

"Cassandra," a voice said behind her.

She stopped moving but didn't turn around.

"Where are you going?" Arphaxad said tightly.

She drew in a deep breath and let it out again. She didn't want to do this. Not with him. Not right now. "Home," she said.

"Now?" His voice was tinged with confusion and frustration.

"There's nothing more for me to do here," she said shortly.

"You really think that's true?" His voice was flat, but the simmering disappointment behind it was tangible.

Cassandra's fingers clenched, and she swallowed hard against the lump rising in her throat. She wanted so badly to tell him no, to turn around and follow him back into that room, to work side by side like they had in the enclave. But no good would come of it. Not for her, and not for Rendra. She had already overstayed her welcome. "Yes," she said firmly, the broken pieces of her heart scattering to the wind. "I do."

Silence stretched out behind her, and she wanted to turn around and shake him and scream at him and let him hold her while she sobbed that it was all so unfair.

"You'll need this," he said. She heard him fiddle with something, and she turned to see him pull a dagger from his belt and hold it out to her. "Take it."

She hesitated a moment, and he sighed. "Don't be stupid, Cass," he said. Then, "Careful. There's briar root in the handle."

A lump formed in her throat, and she took it slowly, careful not to meet his gaze. The hilt was still warm from his hand. She sheathed it silently in one of the open slots on her belt, next to the dagger Karim had given her.

He stepped back, and his face was blank, devoid even of the infuriating arrogance she was so used to seeing there.

"Thank you for your help," he said blandly, his eyes focused somewhere in the middle distance.

"Thank you too," she returned, her voice equally stiff. Her heart was shattering into a million tiny pieces. But it was stupid, stupid, stupid. She would get over it. She had to get over it.

Castez had been informed of Amanakar's treachery. He and Arphaxad were already putting together a plan of action. Medira would know in due time and would deal with the ambassador. She wasn't needed here anymore. Her duty was to Rendra.

There was a village at the head of the Malathi pass she could make it to before nightfall, a contact she could take refuge with. She was the queen's shadow. She could disappear into the forest, where not even Arphaxad Ilin Serra could find her.

A dull ache settled in her chest. Before she could think better of it, she turned away from him, crossed the ragged cobblestones of the courtyard, and walked out the gate.

Chapter 9

Cassandra made it back to Rendra in less than a week, her body crumpling with exhaustion. She wrote a comprehensive report as the queen had requested, and when she was finished, she curled up in bed and slept the rest of the day.

She had succeeded in her mission. She had uncovered Amanakar's plan. Medira would be warned, and Ineti. Rendra and Medira would find common ground for an alliance. Arphaxad would marry the Inetian princess. Peace would reign.

So why did she feel so empty?

She tried not to remember the way Arphaxad had looked at her in the woods above the enclave. She tried not to remember the feel of his body against hers as he'd shielded her from the cave collapse, and the warmth of his breath as she'd huddled in his arms, feeling safer than she ever had before. Those memories could never mean anything at all.

"I know something's wrong," the queen said when she came to Cassandra's room three days later.

"Nothing's wrong," Cassandra said gloomily. "I'm just tired."

The queen watched her, her lips pressed together. Cassandra avoided her gaze. Elena knew her better than anyone.

"You've been through a lot this week, Cassandra," her sister said softly. "But there's something you're not telling me."

A lump rose in Cassandra's throat. She wasn't ready to talk about this with anyone. Not now. Maybe not ever.

"But if you won't tell me, I can't help you," her sister continued. "What I do know is that you can't keep yourself shut up in here forever."

"I can't?" Cassandra said, her voice coming out more bitter than she'd intended.

"No," the queen said. "You cannot. Whatever happened, you are stronger than that. You're the queen's shadow."

And so, Cassandra had gotten up.

She went about her duties in a haze. Some days she practiced archery for hours—but even that was a reminder of the bow she'd lost, of him. Some days she attended court with the queen, standing in her place behind her sister in the formal deep-blue cape of the queen's shadow. She was thankful for the depth of the hood—that way no one could see her face.

Some days she laid in bed until noon, fighting back nightmares of a black clawing nothingness that threatened to consume her whole, but those were becoming fewer and far between. The queen was right. She was more than this malaise. She was the queen's shadow. She could act like it.

She dutifully went through the information coming from her contacts about Medira and Ineti, expecting to hear of the wedding any day. But an alliance and a royal wedding took a long time to plan. Even so, the information was eerily silent.

She did manage to gather that Medira had led a force into the enclave and that the rogue Inetians had been thwarted. The enclave's status in Medira was still to be determined, and the Inetians had not been released to the emperor. There was an ongoing discussion between the two nations as to their fate. Amanakar had been placed under house arrest. Cassandra's mouth had twisted at that particular news, which Isabel, her best agent, had brought after traveling two days and nights without rest so Cassandra would be the first to know.

The queen had taken this information in stride, as well as Cassandra's story of what had happened at the enclave. Cassandra had glossed over most of what had happened between her and Arphaxad, and the queen had narrowed her eyes but hadn't pressed her further. It was just as well. Cassandra might have broken and told her everything.

Most nights, she laid her daggers out on the stand beside her bed: her own, the handle worn and faded; the one Arphaxad had given her when she'd fled the outpost, with its sharp blade; and the one Karim had used to free them, its black handle etched with the golden bird of Ineti. Rendra, Medira, Ineti. She wondered what had happened to Karim, if he'd survived the raid. Memories swirled in her mind, and she tried her best to push them away.

One morning, not long after the news of the enclave raid, Cassandra couldn't find Tomas at his post. When she asked, the queen said airily that he had gone home to his sick mother in the north of Rendra. Cassandra hoped circumstances weren't too dire.

The days passed in a haze. The summer heat gave way to the cooler nights of autumn. The soft patter of rain was more often heard on the black tile roof of the palace.

One such afternoon, Cassandra pushed open the door to her room and froze, her fingers still resting on the handle. There in the corner, leaning against the white stucco wall, was a bow. Her heart thudded as she stared at the familiar curve of the wood. It wasn't just any bow—it was *her* bow, the one that had been a gift from the queen. The one that had been taken from her at the enclave. The one she'd thought she'd never see again.

Her pulse quickened, and she took a careful step back, her eyes darting around the room for any sign of forced entry. But everything was as she'd left it—the bedsheets still crumpled, her nightdress draped hastily over the back of her desk chair, the stack of unopened correspondence that had been left on her desk that morning by a porter untouched. She moved hurriedly into the room and rifled through the letters, but nothing seemed to be missing.

Her bow. She swallowed hard as she stared at it, a gyre of emotions raging through her. There was only one person who could have left it like this. But that was impossible.

There was a knock on the door, and Cassandra jumped. She balked in surprise as her sister entered. Elena was dressed in her formal court gown, resplendent in gold and white, the sleeves embroidered with delicate roses. The heavy crown of Rendra was twined into her graying hair, which was bound up in an elegant knot.

"I need you to attend me in the throne room immediately," the queen said without preamble. "An envoy from Medira has arrived."

"What?" Cassandra said more sharply than she had intended. Her eyes slid to her bow as her pulse spiked. "From Medira?"

The queen nodded. "A foray into a formal alliance."

Arphaxad's promise. She blinked. She hadn't been as attentive as she should have been lately, but her network hadn't even brought her whispers of this. She realized she hadn't seen Isabel since the day she'd brought the news of the enclave raid, which was unusual.

"You knew about this?" she demanded.

"Of course." The queen didn't quite meet Cassandra's eyes. "I requested it."

"Without consulting me?" As the queen's shadow, she should have been the first to know.

"You haven't been yourself," the queen said pointedly.

Guilt tugged at her chest. "I know but—"

"Just be there," the queen cut her off, then turned and left the room.

A heady mix of excitement and terror twined in her chest as she donned the deep blue cape of the queen's shadow. She cast another wild look at her bow, hardly daring to hope at what it might mean.

When she entered the throne room, the queen was already seated, as were her most trusted advisors and a few high-ranking officials. Cassandra slipped to her place at the back of the hall just behind the throne where the queen sat, tension winding through her like a cord about to snap.

The whispers around the room ceased as the door to the throne room opened, and Tomas entered, followed by the Mediran envoy. Cassandra blinked. Wasn't he supposed to be on leave to help his sick mother?

As the envoy made its way down the length of the hall, Cassandra found her eyes roving down the line of Medirans dressed in red and green regalia, telling herself that she wouldn't be disappointed, that it was impossible, that the bow didn't mean anything, that she was fine.

Then she saw him. He moved lithely behind the man dressed in the formal robes of ambassador—a tall, slim figure, so terribly, achingly familiar.

Her feet rooted to the floor, and her heart pounded painfully in her chest. What was he doing here? Shouldn't he be squirreled away in Medira, readying himself to marry his princess? This couldn't be real.

"Galatan Ilin Remada, Lord of Medira, and acting ambassador to Rendra," the chamberlain announced.

The ambassador and the rest of the envoys bowed as they reached the queen. As much as she tried, Cassandra couldn't keep her eyes off Arphaxad. He was dressed in an unassuming black tunic, far less ostentatious than the rest of the envoys, and she could see the nondescript belt around his waist that was glaringly devoid of the daggers that usually hung there. His hair was shorter than it had been when she'd last seen him, trimmed close around his ears. All traces of the stubbly beard were gone, and his arm was no longer in its sling.

Her heart gave a panicked thud. He was *here*. Why was he *here*?

As he rose from his bow, his eyes lifted in her direction. Heat flooded her body as their gazes collided, the intensity in it thundering down to her toes. He gave her a nod before turning back to face the queen.

Cassandra's world was tilting. She hardly heard a word exchanged between the queen and the ambassador. It was mostly formal greetings anyway, but Cassandra didn't care. He was here, in the same room, not off with his Inetian princess. And the way he had looked at her—Cassandra shivered. She tried not to let her mind wander back to the Malathi pass, to the memories she'd tried so hard to force down, to the fire he lit in her veins.

Cassandra hardly saw what gifts were offered to the queen, what words were spoken in flowery placation. She could hardly think at all, let alone focus on what was happening in front of her.

Time slowed to a viscous ooze, and she couldn't keep her eyes off him, so she tried to watch the ceiling or the obsidian and quartz of the floor beneath her feet. With a start, she realized that staring at the floor likely wasn't polite to a visiting ambassador, and so she jerked her head up, only to find Arphaxad grinning at her, and she couldn't help but grin stupidly back.

Then the audience was over, and the envoys were turning around and marching back out of the throne room. Arphaxad caught her gaze one more time, and heat blazed through her body again, before he turned and followed the ambassador out the tall doors.

The queen rose, and her advisors rose with her, waiting until she nodded in dismissal before filing out the doors themselves. The queen cast a glance at Cassandra.

"Go," she said, and her mouth turned up in a rare smile.

"What?" Cassandra said dumbly, staring at her sister.

"I said go. Go find him."

"You—" Cassandra started. Her mouth opened and closed but no more sound came out.

"I'm your sister, Cassandra. I'm not an idiot."

And then Cassandra was moving, fire roaring through her veins as she flew down the corridor behind the throne room and around the corner. She collided with someone in the hallway, and then strong arms were steadying her, setting her back on her feet.

"Cass?"

She leaped backward as if she'd been shot from a catapult, heat flooding her cheeks. "Phax," she choked out, staring up at him.

"You—" he started at the same time that she said, "I didn't—"

They both broke off, staring awkwardly at each other.

"What are you doing here?" she blurted, unable to tear her gaze away from his. He looked good. Really, *really* good. "You're not married to the Inetian princess?"

"No," he said vehemently. His eyes flashed. "I'm certainly not."

Arphaxad ran his fingers through his hair, then glanced at the corridor around them. They weren't alone by any means. A few of the queen's ladies-in-waiting brushed by them, casting them snide looks. A porter bustled by with a bag thrown over his shoulder. "Can we— Is there somewhere we can go?" he said. "To talk?"

"To talk," Cassandra repeated dumbly, her gaze traveling down the corridor as she tried to squash her brain back into her head. "There's a small study around the corner. It's not used much."

He followed her down the hall, and his presence beside her was exhilarating, terrifying, as if she were on a precipice, a terrifying unknown stretched out below her. They rounded the corner, and the gilded door of the study came into view. Her hands were shaking as she fumbled with the doorknob, but it finally turned, and then they were inside, and he was closing the door behind them.

She waited until he turned around, but her head was a blank space that she couldn't quite seem to fill. She had to get a hold of herself.

"Cass, I—" he said at the same time that she said, "You—"

They both stopped again.

"You're here with the Mediran envoys," she said stupidly. "I didn't know you were coming, or else I would have . . ." She trailed off. Or else she'd have what? Ignored a direct order from the queen and refused to come to the throne room? Avoided the Mediran envoys for the rest of the week?

"The whole thing was a little last minute," he said.

"Elena only told me right before you all arrived and—" She cut herself off, embarrassment tinging her cheeks again.

They stared at each other.

"Did you get my gift?" he said in a rush.

She swallowed, her mind rushing to catch up with his words before she managed, "I did."

"Good." He smirked.

She almost rolled her eyes, but it turned into an incredulous smile. "Where— How did you get it back?"

He rubbed his bad shoulder absently. "I—I'm sure you heard that we raised a force to raid the enclave."

She nodded. "I did."

"It went better than we expected. We managed to apprehend the Inetians before they could work any of their newly learned magic, which, it seems, they weren't adept enough to employ quickly enough to be of any use." His mouth twisted. "It turns out that most of the enclave didn't want anything to do with the Inetians after what happened in the cave."

Cassandra snorted. She wasn't surprised.

"That single mistake wiped out a decade of work," he continued. "Doors of that size and complexity aren't simple to build and take an enormous amount of power and time to make properly."

Cassandra ground her teeth. It had all been because of greed and power. Amanakar was full of himself, but the enclave wasn't without fault either.

Arphaxad watched her closely. "It seems the deal was struck with the Inetians by a few chanters in power within the enclave. It was a decision that was forced on the rest of them."

Cassandra's mind skittered to the white-haired chanter, Gustav, and how he'd snarled at her that there were things she could never understand. She understood what it was like to be unwanted. To not be acknowledged for who you were, like Gustav, like the chanters. But it hadn't driven her to madness—and she supposed she had Elena to thank for that, and Andre.

"We apprehended a few of the chanters who sided with the Inetians, but it was a bit . . . explosive." He grimaced. "Some of them surrendered and some of them just . . . disappeared."

Cassandra's heart dipped. She didn't doubt that the white-haired chanter had been one who had slipped away. She couldn't see him surrendering to Medira ever.

"Anyway," he continued. "I found your bow during the raid."

"You didn't have to do that," she said around the lump in her throat. He was glossing over how much extra effort it must have been to find it amid the chaos, to save it, to bring it back to the Mediran palace, and then all the way to Rendra.

"I wanted to," he said softly. He fiddled with one of the loops where his daggers usually were on his belt, then glanced at the empty hearth at one end of the room, then back toward her. "I, just... That day at the outpost—why did you leave? Without saying anything. After all that."

After all that. Her heart twisted painfully. "What else was I supposed to do?" she said miserably. "I was redundant. It was better that I just disappeared."

"Not for me," he said. Her head jerked up, the intensity in his voice sending shivers down her spine.

"You were supposed to marry the Inetian princess," she burst out.

"I know," he said. He crossed his arms and then uncrossed them. An extra movement. A nervous tick she wasn't used to seeing from him. "I agreed to the king's request that I marry the Inetian princess because it was the right thing to do for Medira. And I had to do *something* to—" He stopped abruptly. "The marriage alliance disintegrated after everything with the enclave. Ineti has too much instability. It's not worth it for Medira." He paused, and his eyes flicked to her face. "But what is worth it for Medira is an alliance with Rendra."

She didn't dare move. "An alliance," she said.

"An alliance," he repeated. Another shiver moved down her spine.

"Tomas came to me last week with a proposal from the queen," he continued.

"Tomas did?" Cassandra's mind reeled. So, her sister had lied when she'd said that Tomas was with his sick mother. The sneak.

"Yes," Arphaxad said. "Luckily, it was the same conclusion I was coming to on my own, but they ... helped move me along."

Cassandra's pulse hammered in her throat. She couldn't allow herself to hope that he was about to say what she thought he was.

"It would be good for Medira and Rendra if there was a marriage alliance," he plowed on. "And since I was the previous candidate with Ineti, it seemed like a good idea if I were again, but with Rendra." He absently reached for the daggers that weren't there on his belt, then stopped when he realized what he was doing. "And I would come to live here and help with your information network. I already have someone primed as my successor in Medira. And you know how I feel about working for my king anyway."

Cassandra stared at him, trying to push her brain to catch up with the words that were coming out of his mouth. An alliance. He was offering an alliance.

"Damn it," he said, turning away from her and pacing to the wall. "I'm not saying this very well."

"You're—you're doing fine," Cassandra said. "I—don't stop now."

He turned back to face her, his eyes glowing. "What I'm trying to say, Cass," he continued, "is that I love you." For once, he sounded unsure of himself—not unsure of the words, but unsure of her response. "I have for a long time. I can't get you out of my head. Every time I thought I might run into you on a mission, I went for it. Damn it, I was hoping I would find you at the enclave and I did." His mouth tilted. "You're witty and intelligent and beautiful and you drive me absolutely insane, but I love every part of it. Of you."

Cassandra couldn't look away, couldn't believe the words that were coming out of his mouth.

"I tried so hard to forget you," he said. "And then there you were, doing your best to snark your way through an entire enclave of chanters and rogue Inetians. And I was completely lost."

He took a step toward her, energy snapping between them. Her mind was a blank, her emotions whirling in a heightened twister of want and elation and disbelief. He was in love with her. After everything. He wanted her, just as much as she wanted him.

"Cass," he said. "I—will you marry me?"

Cassandra's pulse thundered in her ears, and she opened her mouth, but he hurried on. "Please don't say yes out of obligation to the queen. I only want you to say yes if it's what you actually want."

"Yes," she said, almost before he had stopped speaking.

"Yes?" He looked as stunned as she felt.

"Yes," she said. She didn't know what to do with her hands or her feet or her body. What had she been doing with them all this time anyway?

"You're sure?" he said, taking another step toward her, his face lighting up like a puppy's.

"Yes, you dimwit," she snapped, but she couldn't keep a stupid grin from sliding across her face.

Now Arphaxad was grinning too. He reached out his hand, his eyes wide as if he couldn't believe what was happening. His thumb slid along her jaw just as it had that evening in the forest above the enclave. Cassandra's breath hitched sharply. "This is where we left off, wasn't it?" he said, his voice rough.

"I think so," Cassandra whispered. Tension vibrated in every sinew of her body. "What was it you were planning to do next?"

"I had a few thoughts." He grinned, his fingers sliding along her jaw and moving to cup the back of her neck.

"I love you," she said, because she realized she hadn't said it yet.

His breath hitched, and then he was kissing her, pulling her body flush against him, and her hands twined around his neck, her fingers tangling in his hair, just like she'd pretended she hadn't thought about doing every time she'd ever seen him, and he was tracing along her back with his fingers, and she never wanted it to end.

This. This was everything she had ever dreamed of. The thing she'd thought was impossible. And now he was here, and he was *hers*, and she couldn't understand how it had happened. Just that morning, she had been mired in the wall of malaise, trying her best to forget him and to move on.

Her heart soared. There were still so many things to talk through, to iron out, between politics and roles and what Medira would get and what Rendra wanted and her ridiculous, wonderful, amazing sister and her schemes, but this, here, with him, this was what mattered.

"We should probably go tell the queen," Cassandra said after a time—she wasn't sure how long—pulling back so she could look up at him.

"Not right now we aren't." He spread his hand against the small of her back and pressed her closer against him. "I'm not planning on letting go of you anytime soon."

She had no desire to argue. She leaned up and kissed him again. He laughed against her mouth, a sound of pure joy, as he deepened the kiss, his hands sliding up her back and into her hair.

This was joy and love and belonging. There was an alliance to build and an emperor to placate and an enclave to find a home for, but they would face them in time, together. For now, the other things could wait.

Epilogue

The wedding was a spectacle.

Cassandra wore a dress dripping with white lace and pale blue trim, with a train so long she was sure she would trip on it. One of the queen's ladies-in-waiting had spent half the morning doing Cassandra's thick hair in an elaborate coif, festooned with pearls and sapphires.

"You'll be fine," the queen said as they waited not far from the throne room for the ceremony to begin. The queen was dressed in an elegant gown of gold and pearl, her hair piled high on her head, the crown of Rendra sitting regally on top. *She* had no ridiculous train to contend with.

"What if someone attacks me?" Cassandra said petulantly. "How am I supposed to get to my daggers without ripping the whole thing apart?"

The queen's brow rose. "Please don't tell me you have a dagger on you on your wedding day."

"Daggers," she couldn't help correcting.

The queen gave her a look, but there was a hint of amusement in her gaze. "No one is going to attack you," she said. "We've spent weeks making sure of that."

"You never know," Cassandra muttered. "Two sovereigns in one place and all that."

After much cajoling, the Mediran king had deigned to attend a wedding he had greatly desired not to take place in Rendra. Cassandra thought he would have accepted an unreasonably remote, snow-laden island in the southern sea beyond the Alliance lands just on principle. There had been a long back and forth between the two nations about the wedding arrangements and the exact terms of the alliance, which had tired Cassandra to no end. The queen had been patient—incredibly patient—with a man who clearly couldn't see beyond his own bulging nose. Now, more than ever, she understood Arphaxad's exasperation with the king and his position.

"We will come to an agreement," the queen had told Cassandra after a particularly irritating exchange. "This should have happened a long time ago. Our peninsula needs this."

Cassandra snorted. "You are a much kinder person than I am."

"I don't know about that. I just hide it better." Her mouth quirked. "Besides, you *want* to marry Arphaxad, if the way you moon around after him is any indication."

"I do not moon," Cassandra protested weakly. The queen was right about one thing: she very much did want to marry Arphaxad. And she *might* have been a bit of a puddle lately whenever he was around. She was also becoming increasingly convinced that they should just drop the whole ridiculous elaborate wedding and elope somewhere where no one would bother them.

The bright sound of horns and stringed instruments threaded through the doorway, indicating the start of the procession. Cassandra's body thrummed with a mix of fear and excitement. It was happening. She was getting *married.*

As soon as the doors opened, her gaze snapped to Arphaxad standing at the head of the throne room, and the rest of the pageantry and fanfare faded away. He was dressed in a fitted green tunic trimmed with red and gold. His boots were black and rose almost to his knee. She thought she could detect the outline of a dagger in each one. His eyes widened when he saw her, and she couldn't help the giddy grin that slid across her face.

The walk toward the throne at the end of the room felt like an eternity. She paced slowly beside her sister, trying not to trip on her train, while music played and a full gallery of elaborately dressed courtiers and ministers looked on.

"The wedding is going to have to be as extravagant as possible," Arphaxad had said with a grimace a few weeks before. "We're making a statement that this is not an alliance that is to be trifled with. People are going to expect pomp and circumstance."

Cassandra had made a face. She knew he was right. It wasn't every day that the Rendran queen's sister married the Mediran king's nephew.

The news that the queen's shadow was the old king's daughter had come as a shock to most of Rendra. But the queen's dogged insistence of Cassandra's rights as the king's daughter and Arphaxad's sharp comments whenever someone questioned her position or said something snide had quickly silenced the naysayers. At least in her presence. She had spent years at court building her reputation as the queen's shadow. She had enough clout for most people to accept her, if not with enthusiasm, at least with hopeful skepticism.

The rest of the ceremony passed in a blur. She stood side by side with Arphaxad, her body burgeoning with tension, as they repeated the ancient vows that had been part of the royal marriage ceremony for generations.

And then it was over, and they were recessing arm in arm out of the throne room, past the dark, pouting face of the Mediran king and the polite smiles of Arphaxad's parents—who had turned out to be reserved but kind—and the sly grin of his younger brother, and out into the glittering sunlight in the courtyard beneath a brilliant blue sky. Out beyond the palace, Cassandra could make out the snow-capped peaks of the Malathi pass. Her heart squeezed. If it hadn't been for the rogue Inetians and the enclave, she wouldn't be here today, standing hand in hand with Arphaxad Ilin Serra, the entire world before them.

A gilded carriage pulled by eight white horses—exactly as Cassandra had once imagined a fitting conveyance for a queen—was waiting for them at the bottom of the steps, and Cassandra almost rolled her eyes at the extravagance. She allowed Arphaxad to help her in, dragging that ridiculous train in behind her so that it pooled like a lake of white around her feet. Arphaxad climbed in behind her and shut the door firmly behind them. The carriage had hardly started moving when he enthusiastically pulled her against him and kissed her.

A giggle bubbled up from her belly, and she pulled away briefly to grin at him. "Wasting no time, I see."

"Now that we're married, absolutely not," he said.

"Don't we have a party to attend after this?"

He groaned. "I was hoping we could skip it." He trailed a few kisses along her jaw, his fingers tightening at her waist. And now she really, really wanted to skip it too.

"Wasn't it you who declared our wedding was to be as extravagant as possible?" she said with a grin. "An absolute spectacle. For the sake of the alliance."

"You can be insufferable, you know," he said against her neck. She could hear the smile in his voice.

"I don't think I'm alone in that," she whispered.

She kissed him the rest of the way to the gala and didn't care that her hair had fallen down.

READ THE NEXT BOOK IN THE SERIES

THE SHADOW'S EDGE: THE CHANTERS NOVELLAS 2

He's a traitor to his crown. She's the only one who can save him.

Isabel Algerin just wanted to serve her queen. She didn't intend to break Karim Saad, a traitor to the powerful Inetian empire, out of prison. And she certainly didn't intend for him to awaken her unpredictable shadow magic—the magic she'd tried her whole life to hide.

But with a dark mage hunting them and an enemy army in close pursuit, Isabel and Karim are flung into a dangerous game of magic and intrigue that leaves them scrambling for their lives. As they try to untangle the powerful new magic surging between them, they will also have to untangle their growing feelings for each other—and what that might mean in a world teetering on the edge of shadow.

Available on Amazon.com or rachelsongauthor.com

Sign up for my newsletter on rachelsongauthor.com

Acknowledgements

Thank you to my wonderful husband Michael Song, for his unending support and for pushing me to be better at everything I do. You're my alpha reader and my copy editor. Thank you for putting up with me as I talk through plot holes and go on tangents about characters.

I would not be the writer I am today without the amazing ladies of my critique group, Abigail Ford and Michelle Dobson. You guys are full of knowledge, wit, and hilarity, and aren't afraid to give me honest and much-needed feedback, as well as pep talks to get me out of a writing slump! Our frenzied, endless evenings of writing sprints have pushed me to get more words out with more consistency than I ever imagined possible. You've laughed and cried and fangirled over my writing, and I could not have done this without you.

I also want to extend a thank you to my mentor in all things editing, writing, and publishing related, Pamela Gossiaux. You believed in me when I had no direction, showing me that I could make a career out of my passion for writing. You've been endlessly helpful with your knowledge of the publishing industry and what it takes to get a book out there!

And finally, thank you to my parents, Steven and Monika Lamine, for encouraging me in all my endeavors, allowing me to read and write and travel the world to my heart's content.

ABOUT THE AUTHOR

Rachel Song is a fantasy romance author and fiction editor, and has been an avid writer and reader since she was eight years old. She remembers gleefully huddling under the covers with a forbidden flashlight, reading until the wee hours of the morning. Some of her favorite authors include Jane Austen, Juliet Marillier, VE Schwab, Sherwood Smith, Megan Whalen Turner, Garth Nix, and J.R.R Tolkien.

Rachel lives with her husband and son in metro-Detroit, where, when not writing, she can be found reading, cooking, gardening, traveling, and playing something adventurous on her PS5.

She is the author of *The Chanters Novellas* series, and you can learn more about her and her books on rachelsongauthor.com.

Made in the USA
Columbia, SC
28 June 2024